DJUNA

Nightwood

ff
faber and faber

First published in 1936
by Faber and Faber Limited
3 Queen Square London WC1N 3AU
Faber Library edition published 1996
This paperback edition with new introduction first published in 2007

Printed in England by Bookmarque, Croydon

A CIP record for this book
is available from the British Library

ISBN 978–0–571–23528–5

ISBN 0–571–23528–X

2 4 6 8 10 9 7 5 3 1

NIGHTWOOD

Djuna Barnes was born in 1892 in Cornwall-on-Hudson in New York State. She studied art and worked as a journalist in New York before moving to Paris in the twenties. Her other works include *The Book of Repulsive Women* (1915), *Ladies Almanack* (1928), *Ryder* (1928), the verse play *The Antiphon* (1958), and collections of journalism, interviews and short stories. She returned to Greenwich Village in 1940 and died there in 1982.

or

To
Peggy Guggenheim
and
John Ferrar Holmes

Contents

Introduction

Certain texts work in homeopathic dilutions; that is, nano-amounts effect significant change over long periods of time.

Nightwood is a nano-text.

It is, in any case, not much more than a couple of hundred pages long, and more people have heard about it than have read it. Reading it is mainly the preserve of academics and students. Others have a vague sense that it is a modernist text, that T. S. Eliot adored it, that Dylan Thomas called it 'one of the three major prose works by a woman' (accept the compliment to D.B., ignore the insult directed elsewhere), that the work is an important milestone on any map of gay literature – even though, like all the best books, its power makes a nonsense of any categorization, especially of gender or sexuality.

Nightwood is itself. It is its own created world, exotic and strange, and reading it is like drinking wine with a pearl dissolving in the glass. You have taken in more than you know, and it will go on doing its work. From now on, a part of you is pearl-lined.

In his Preface, Eliot talks about the necessity of reading *Nightwood* more than once – because the second reading will feel very different to the first. This is true.

In our society, where it is hard to find time to do anything properly, even once, the leisure, which is part of the pleasure of reading, is one of our culture-casualties.

For us, books have turned into fast food, to be consumed in the gaps between one bout of relentless living and the next. Airports, subways, maybe half an hour at bedtime, maybe something with the office sandwich, isn't really ideal. At least at the cinema, or at the theatre, or at a concert, or even in a gallery, some real time has to be set aside. Books have been squeezed in, which goes a long way towards explaining why our appetite for literature is waning, and our allergic reaction to anything demanding is on the rise.

Nightwood is demanding. You can slide into it, because the prose has a narcotic quality, but you can't slide over it. The language is not about conveying information; it is about conveying meaning. There is much more to this book than its story, which is slight, or even its characters, who are magnificent tricks of the light. This is not the solid nineteenth-century world of narrative; it is the shifting, slipping, relative world of Einstein and the modernists, the twin assault by science and art on what we thought we were sure of.

That is why, in *Nightwood*, Baron Felix represents a world that is disappearing. It is why he is so confused about the world he must live in, and why his son Guido is a kind of holy fool. As Gertrude Stein put it so well, 'There is no there there.' You can read this twice – as a comment on matter, and a warning against consolation.

There is no consolation in *Nightwood*. There is a wild intensity, recklessness, defiance in the face of suffering. All the characters are exiles of one kind or another – Americans, Irish, Austrian, Jewish. This is the beginning of the modern diaspora – all peoples, all places, all change.

Djuna Barnes's 1920s/1930s Paris is a Paris on the cusp of leaving behind forever the *haute* world of Henry James, taken from Proust. That is a world where the better people dine in the Bois, and where open horse-drawn carriages still circle the park. It is in this world that the eager hands of Jenny Petheridge first claw at Robin Vote, the American whom we meet passed out dead drunk in one of the new class of 'middle' hotels, designed for a new kind of tourist – definitely not of the old world of servants and steamer trunks.

Seedy Paris of whores and cheap bars has not yet begun to change. It is to this world that Robin Vote is drawn; the night-time world, where she will not be judged, and where she can find the anonymity of a stranger's embrace. This world is faithfully tracked and searched by Robin's lover, Norah Flood, hunting faint imprints of her errant *amour*, sometimes finding her, collapsed with drink, and threatened by police, beggars, and women on the make.

It is a bleak picture of love between women. Jenny Petheridge avid and ruthless: 'When she fell in love it was with a perfect fury of accumulated dishonesty; she became instantly a dealer in second-hand and therefore incalculable emotions . . . she appropriated the most passionate love that she knew, Nora's for Robin. She was a squatter by instinct.'

Nora Flood: 'I have been loved', she said, 'by something strange, and it has forgotten me.'

Robin Vote 'sitting with her legs thrust out. Her hair thrown back against the embossed cushions of the chair, sleeping, one arm fallen over the chair's side, the hand somehow older and wiser than her body'.

Robin's passivity, Jenny's predatory nature, and Nora's passionate devotion make an impossible triangle. The daily assaults of selfishness and self-harm do not offer a picture of love between women as anything safe or easy. A negative reading would sink us into the misery of the 'invert'; the medical pathology of Havelock Ellis, and the bitterness of Radclyffe Hall and *The Well of Loneliness* (1928).

Djuna Barnes was well aware of these readings, and her own Paris community had its fair share of destroyed lives – think of Renee Vivian or Dolly Wilde. Djuna Barnes had spoofed the gay and not-so-gay times of her circle in *Ladies Almanack*, but if she was able to lampoon it – and that in itself is much healthier than Radclyffe Hall's miserable mopings – then she was also able to celebrate it.

Nightwood has neither stereotypes nor caricatures; there is a truth to these damaged hearts that moves us beyond the negative. Humans suffer and, gay or straight, they break themselves into pieces, blur themselves with drink and drugs, choose the wrong lover, crucify themselves on their own longings, and, let's not forget, are crucified by a world that fears the stranger – whether in life or in love.

In *Nightwood*, they are all strangers, and they speak to those of us who are always, or just sometimes, the stranger; or to the ones who open the door to find the stranger standing outside.

And yet, there is great dignity in Nora's love for Robin, written without cliché or compromise in the full-blown, archetypal language of romance. We are left in no doubt that this love is worthy of greatness – that it is great. As the doctor, Matthew O'Connor remarks, 'Nora will leave that girl some day; but though those two are buried at the opposite ends of the earth, one dog will find them both.'

'Grave' would have been a cliché; 'dog' is a snapping stroke of genius. That's how alive is the language of this text.

Robin, Nora, Jenny. Robin's brief and disastrous marriage to Baron Felix, Felix's own story of inferiority and loss, the underworld life of Paris are all seen through the glittering eyes of a creature half-leprechaun, half-angel, half-freak, half-savant, half-man, half-woman: the 'doctor', Matthew-Mighty-grain-of-salt-Dante-O'Connor.

It is the doctor who first finds Robin Vote drowned in drink; the doctor who becomes the confidante of Felix, and urges him to carry his son's mind 'like a bowl picked up in the dark; you do not know what is in it'.

It is the doctor who talks his way through life as though words were a needle and thread that could mend it. When Nora finally comes to him, in the blackness of her despair, he talks her through it, alright, sitting up in his tiny iron bed, in a servant's room at the top of a house, the slop bucket to one side, 'brimming with abominations'.

The doctor is wearing full make-up, a nightgown and a woman's wig – he had been expecting someone else, but he begins his speech, as good as Molly Bloom's soliloquy in *Ulysses*, and this episode is a linguistic, artistic and emotional triumph. It matters that it is emotional. *Nightwood* is not afraid of feeling. It is not a glittering high-wire act; its pearls are deep-dived, and then dissolved into the language.

The best texts are time-machines; they are of their moment, and can tell it, and they can take us back there later. But they are something more too – they live on into the future because they were never strapped into time.

Most of what we hype is time-bound, and soon vanishes. Indeed, a good test of a work of art is that it goes on interesting us long after any contemporary relevance is dead. We don't go to Shakespeare to find out about life in Elizabethan England; we go to Shakespeare to find out about ourselves now.

Djuna Barnes's Paris is of its moment, but *Nightwood* has not survived as a slice of history, but as a work of art. The excitements and atmosphere of her period are there, but there is nothing locked-in about *Nightwood*.

Readers in 1936, when *Nightwood* was published in Britain, would have been uncomfortably aware of Hitler's rise and rise, and his notorious propaganda offensive at the Berlin Olympic Games – remember 'Joy Through Strength'?

It was the year of the Abdication Crisis, when Edward VIII chose his American mistress, Wallace Simpson, over the English throne.

In America, other women were in the headlines – Margaret Mitchell published *Gone With the Wind*, and Clare Luce Booth's stageplay *The Women* was taking Broadway by storm. This year also saw the start of the Spanish Civil War.

Nightwood isn't directly connected to any of this – a good example of why we must be careful of muddling up a work of art, or not a work of art, with its subject matter.

Art isn't rarefied or aloof, but it may have different concerns to the general – for instance, the Napoleonic Wars are never mentioned by Jane Austen, although she was living and working right through them.

Nightwood, peculiar, eccentric, particular, shaded against the insistence of too much daylight, is a book for introverts, in that we are all introverts in our after-hours secrets and deepest loves.

Our world, this one now, wants everything on the outside, displayed and confessed, but really it cannot be so. The private dialogue of reading is an old-fashioned confessional, and better for it. What you admit here, what the book admits to you, is between you both and left there. *Nightwood* is a place where much can be said – and left unsaid.

For the rest of my life I will be climbing those stairs with Nora to the doctor's filthy garret.

Why? Something of *Nightwood* has lodged in me.

It is not my story, or my experience; it is not my voice or my fear. It is, through its language, a true-shot arrow, a wound that is also a remedy. *Nightwood* opens a place that does not easily skin over.

There is pain in who we are, and the pain of love – because love itself is an opening and a wound – is a pain no one escapes except by escaping life itself.

Nightwood is not an escape-text. It writes into the centre of human anguish, unrelieved, but in its dignity and its defiance, it becomes by strange alchemy its own salve.

'Is there such extraordinary need of misery to make beauty?' asks the doctor, but the answer is already written: Yes.

JEANETTE WINTERSON, 2007

Preface

When the question is raised, of writing an introduction to a book of a creative order, I always feel that the few books worth introducing are exactly those which it is an impertinence to introduce. I have already committed two such impertinences; this is the third, and if it is not the last no one will be more surprised than myself. I can justify this preface only in the following way. One is liable to expect other people to see, on their first reading of a book, all that one has come to perceive in the course of a developing intimacy with it. I have read *Nightwood* a number of times, in manuscript, in proof, and after publication. What one can do for other readers – assuming that if you read this preface at all you will read it first – is to trace the more significant phases of one's own appreciation of it. For it took me, with this book, some time to come to an appreciation of its meaning as a whole.

In describing *Nightwood* for the purpose of attracting readers to the English edition, I said that it would 'appeal primarily to readers of poetry.' This is well enough for the brevity of advertisement, but I am glad to take this opportunity to amplify it a little. I do not want to suggest that the distinction of the book is primarily verbal, and still less that the astonishing language covers a vacuity of content. Unless the term 'novel' has become too debased to apply, and if it means a book in which living characters are created and shown in significant relationship, this book is a novel. And I do not mean that Miss Barnes's style is 'poetic prose'. But I do mean that most contemporary novels are not really 'written'. They obtain what reality they have largely from an accurate rendering of the noises that human beings currently make in their daily simple needs of communication; and what part of a novel is not composed of these noises consists of a prose which is no more alive than that of a competent newspaper writer or government official. A prose that is altogether alive demands something of the reader that the ordinary novel-reader is not prepared to give. To say that *Nightwood* will appeal primarily to readers of poetry does not mean that is it not a novel, but that it is so good a novel that only sensibilities trained on poetry can wholly appreciate it. Miss Barnes's prose has the prose rhythm that is prose style, and the musical pattern which is not that of verse. This prose rhythm may be more or less complex or elaborate, according to the purposes of the writer; but whether simple or complex, it is what raises the matter to be communicated, to the first intensity.

When I first read the book I found the opening movement rather slow and dragging, until the appearance of the doctor. And throughout the first reading, I was under the impression that it was the doctor alone who gave the book its vitality; and I believed the final chapter to be superfluous. I am now convinced that the final chapter is essential, both dramatically and musically. It was notable, however, that as the other characters, on repeated reading, became alive for me, and while the focus shifted, the figure of the doctor was by no means diminished. On the contrary, he came to take on a different and more profound importance when seen as a constituent of a whole pattern. He ceased to be like the brilliant actor in an otherwise unpersuasively performed play for whose re-entrance one impatiently waits. However in actual life such a character might seem to engross conversation, quench reciprocity, and blanket less voluble people; in the book his role is nothing of the kind. At first we only hear the doctor talking; we do not understand why he talks. Gradually one comes to see that together with his egotism and swagger – doctor Matthew-Mighty-grain-of-salt-Dante O'Connor – he has also a desperate disinterestedness and a deep humility. His humility does not often appear so centrally as in the prodigious scene in the empty church, but it is what throughout gives him his helpless power among the helpless. His monologues, brilliant and witty in themselves as they are, are not dictated by an indifference to other human beings, but on the contrary by a hypersensitive awareness of them. When Nora comes to visit him in the night (*Watchman, What of the Night?*) he perceives at once that the only thing he can do for her ('he was extremely put out, having expected someone else') – the only way to 'save the situation' – is to talk torrentially, even though she hardly takes in anything he says, but reverts again and again to her obsession. It is his revulsion against the strain of squeezing himself dry for other people, and getting no sustenance in return, that sends him raving at the end. *The people in my life who have made my life miserable, coming to me to learn of degradation and the night.* But most of the time he is talking to drown the still small wailing and whining of humanity, to make more supportable its shame and less ignoble its misery.

Indeed, such a character as Dr O'Connor could not be real alone in a gallery of dummies: such a character needs other real, if less conscious, people in order to realize his own reality. I cannot think of any character in the book who has not gone on living in my mind. Felix and his child are oppressively real. Sometimes in a phrase the characters spring to life so suddenly that one is taken aback, as if one had touched a wax-work figure and discovered that it was a live policeman. The doctor says to Nora, *I was doing well enough until you kicked my stone over, and out I came, all moss and eyes.* Robin Vote (the most puzzling of all, because we find her quite real without quite understanding the means by which the author has made her so) is *the vision of an eland coming down an aisle of trees, chapleted with orange-blossoms and bridal veil, a hoof raised in the economy of fear*; and later she has *temples like those of young beasts cutting horns, as if they were sleeping eyes.* Sometimes also a situation, which we had already comprehended loosely, is concentrated into a horror of intensity by a phrase, as when Nora suddenly thinks on seeing the doctor in bed, '*God, children know something they can't tell; they like Red Riding Hood and the wolf in bed!*'

The book is not simply a collection of individual portraits; the characters are all knotted together, as people are in real life, by what we may call chance or destiny, rather than by deliberate choice of each other's company: it is the whole pattern that they form, rather than any individual constituent, that is the focus of interest. We come to know them through their effect on each other, and by what they say to each other about the others. And finally, it ought to be superfluous to observe – but perhaps to anyone reading the book for the first time, it is not superfluous – that the book is not a psychopathic study. The miseries that people suffer through their particular abnormalities of temperament are visible on the surface: the deeper design is that of the human misery and bondage which is universal. In normal lives this misery is mostly concealed; often, what is most wretched of all, concealed from the sufferer more effectively than from the observer. The sick man does not know what is wrong with him; he partly wants to know, and mostly wants to conceal the knowledge from himself. In the Puritan morality that I remember, it was tacitly assumed that if one was thrifty, enterprising, intelligent, practical and prudent in not violating social conventions, one ought to have a happy and 'successful' life. Failure was due to some weakness or perversity peculiar to the individual; but the decent man need have no nightmares. It is now rather more common to assume that all individual misery is the fault of 'society', and is remediable by alterations from without. Fundamentally, the two philosophies, however different they may appear in operation, are the same. It seems to me that all of us, so far as we attach ourselves to created objects and surrender our wills to temporal ends, are eaten by the same worm. Taken in this way, *Nightwood* appears with profounder significance. To regard this group of people as a horrid sideshow of freaks is not only to miss the point, but to confirm our wills and harden our hearts in an inveterate sin of pride.

I should have considered the foregoing paragraph impertinent, and perhaps too pretentious for a preface meant to be a simple recommendation of a book I greatly admire, were it not that one review (at least), intended in praise of the book, has already appeared which would in effect induce the reader to begin with this mistaken attitude. Otherwise, generally, in trying to anticipate a reader's misdirections, one is in danger of provoking him to some other misunderstanding unforeseen. This is a work of creative imagination, not a philosophical treatise. As I said at the beginning, I am conscious of impertinence in introducing the book at all; and to have read a book a good many times does not necessarily put one in the right knowledge of what to say to those who have not yet read it. What I would leave the reader prepared to find is the great achievement of a style, the beauty of phrasing, the brilliance of wit and characterization, and a quality of horror and doom very nearly related to that of Elizabethan tragedy.

T. S. ELIOT, 1937

Note to Second Edition

The foregoing preface, as the reader will have just observed, was written twelve years ago. It appeared only in the American edition of *Nightwood*, which was published by Harcourt, Brace & Co. shortly after the publication of the book by Faber & Faber in London. In reprinting the book, Faber & Faber have thought fit to include this preface, which thus appears for the first time in an English edition.

As my admiration for the book has not diminished, and my only motive for revision would be to remove or conceal evidences of my own immaturity at the time of writing – a temptation which may present itself to any critic reviewing his own words at twelve years' distance – I have thought best to leave unaltered a preface which may still, I hope, serve its original purpose of indicating an approach helpful for the new reader.

T.S.E., 1949

CHAPTER ONE

Bow Down

Early in 1880, in spite of a well-founded suspicion as to the advisability of perpetuating that race which has the sanction of the Lord and the disapproval of the people, Hedvig Volkbein, a Viennese woman of great strength and military beauty, lying upon a canopied bed of a rich spectacular crimson, the valance stamped with the bifurcated wings of the House of Hapsburg, the feather coverlet an envelope of satin on which, in massive and tarnished gold threads, stood the Volkbein arms – gave birth, at the age of forty-five, to an only child, a son, seven days after her physician predicted that she would be taken.

Turning upon this field, which shook to the clatter of morning horses in the street beyond, with the gross splendour of a general saluting the flag, she named him Felix, thrust him from her, and died. The child's father had gone six months previously, a victim of fever. Guido Volkbein, a Jew of Italian descent, had been both a gourmet and a dandy, never appearing in public without the ribbon of some quite unknown distinction tinging his buttonhole with a faint thread. He had been small, rotund, and haughtily timid, his stomach protruding slightly in an upward jutting slope that brought into prominence the buttons of his waistcoat and trousers, marking the exact centre of his body with the obstetric line seen on fruits – the inevitable arc produced by heavy rounds of burgundy, schlagsahne, and beer.

The autumn, binding him about, as no other season, with racial memories, a season of longing and of horror, he had called his weather. Then walking in the Prater he had been seen carrying in a conspicuously clenched fist the exquisite handkerchief of yellow and black linen that cried aloud of the ordinance of 1468, issued by one Pietro Barbo, demanding that, with a rope about its neck, Guido's race should run in the Corso for the amusement of the Christian populace, while ladies of noble birth, sitting upon spines too refined for rest, arose from their seats, and, with the red-gowned cardinals and the Monsignori, applauded with that cold yet hysterical abandon of a people that is at once unjust and happy, the very Pope himself shaken down from his hold on heaven with the laughter of a man who forgoes his angels that he may recapture the beast. This memory and the handkerchief that accompanied it had wrought in Guido (as certain flowers brought to a pitch of florid ecstasy no sooner attain their specific type than they fall into its decay) the sum total of what is the Jew. He had walked, hot, incautious and damned, his eyelids quivering over the thick eyeballs, black with the pain of a participation that, four centuries later, made him a victim, as he felt the echo in his own throat of that cry running the Piazza Montanara long ago, '*Roba vecchia!*' – the degradation by which his people had survived.

Childless at fifty-nine, Guido had prepared out of his own heart for his coming child a heart, fashioned on his own preoccupation, the remorseless homage to nobility, the genuflexion the hunted body makes from muscular contraction, going down before the impending and inaccessible, as before a great heat. It had made Guido, as it was to make his son, heavy with impermissible blood.

And childless he had died, save for the promise that hung at the Christian belt of Hedvig. Guido had lived as all Jews do, who, cut off from their people by accident or choice, find that they must inhabit a world whose constituents, being alien, force the mind to succumb to an imaginary populace. When a Jew dies on a Christian bosom he dies impaled. Hedvig, in spite of her agony, wept upon an outcast. Her body at that moment became the barrier and Guido died against that wall, troubled and alone. In life he had done everything to span the impossible gap; the saddest and most futile gesture of all had been his pretence to a Barony. He had adopted the sign of the cross; he had said that he was an Austrian of an old, almost extinct line, producing, to uphold his story, the most amazing and inaccurate proofs: a coat of arms that he had no right to and a list of progenitors (including their Christian names) who had never existed. When Hedvig came upon his black and yellow handkerchiefs he had said that they were to remind him that one branch of his family had bloomed in Rome.

He had tried to be one with her by adoring her, by imitating her goose-step of a stride, a step that by him adopted, became dislocated and comic. She would have done as much, but sensing something in him blasphemed and lonely, she had taken the blow as a Gentile must – by moving toward him in recoil. She had believed whatever he had told her, but often enough she had asked: 'What is the matter?' – that continual reproach which was meant as a continual reminder of her love. It ran through his life like an accusing voice. He had been tormented into speaking highly of royalty, flinging out encomiums with the force of small water made great by the pressure of a thumb. He had

3

laughed too heartily when in the presence of the lower order of title, as if, by his good nature, he could advance them to some distinction of which they dreamed. Confronted with nothing worse than a general in creaking leather and with the slight repercussion of movement common to military men, who seem to breathe from the inside out, smelling of gunpowder and horse flesh, lethargic yet prepared for participation in a war not yet scheduled (a type of which Hedvig had been very fond), Guido had shaken with an unseen trembling. He saw that Hedvig had the same bearing, the same though more condensed power of the hand, patterned on seizure in a smaller mould, as sinister in its reduction as a doll's house. The feather in her hat had been knife-clean and quivering as if in an heraldic wind; she had been a woman held up to nature, precise, deep-bosomed and gay. Looking at the two he had become confused as if he were about to receive a reprimand, not the officer's, but his wife's.

When she danced, a little heady with wine, the dance floor had become a tactical manoeuvre; her heels came down staccato and trained, her shoulders as conscious at the tips as those which carry the braid and tassels of promotion; the turn of her head held the cold vigilance of a sentry whose rounds are not without apprehension. Yet Hedvig had done what she could. If ever there was a massive chic she had personified it – yet somewhere there had been anxiety. The thing that she had stalked, though she herself had not been conscious of it, was Guido's assurance that he was a Baron. She had believed it as a soldier 'believes' a command. Something in her sensory predicament – upon which she herself would have placed no value – had told her much better. Hedvig had become a Baroness without question.

In the Vienna of Volkbein's day there were few trades that welcomed Jews, yet somehow he had managed, by various deals in household goods, by discreet buying of old masters and first editions and by money changing, to secure for Hedvig a house in the Inner City, to the north overlooking the Prater, a house that, large, dark and imposing, became a fantastic museum of their encounter.

The long rococo halls, giddy with plush and whorled designs in gold, were peopled with Roman fragments, white and disassociated; a runner's leg, the chilly half-turned head of a matron stricken at the bosom, the blind bold sockets of the eyes given a pupil by every shifting shadow so that what they looked upon was an act of the sun. The great salon was of walnut. Over the fireplace hung impressive copies of the Medici shield and, beside them, the Austrian bird.

Three massive pianos (Hedvig had played the waltzes of her time with the masterly stroke of a man, in the tempo of her blood, rapid and rising – that quick mannerliness of touch associated with the playing of the Viennese, who, though pricked with the love of rhythm, execute its demands in the duelling manner) sprawled over the thick dragon's-blood pile of rugs from Madrid. The study harboured two rambling desks in rich and bloody wood. Hedvig had liked things in twos and threes. Into the middle arch of each desk silver-headed brads had been hammered to form a lion, a bear, a ram, a dove, and in their midst a flaming torch. The design was executed under the supervision of Guido who, thinking on the instant, claimed it as the Volkbein field, though it turned out to be a bit of heraldry long since in decline beneath the papal frown. The full length windows (a French touch that Guido thought handsome) overlooking the park were curtained in native velvets and stuffs from Tunis, and the Venetian blinds were of that peculiarly

5

sombre shade of red so loved by the Austrians. Against the panels of oak that reared themselves above the long table and up to the curving ceiling hung life-sized portraits of Guido's claim to father and mother. The lady was a sumptuous Florentine with bright sly eyes and overt mouth. Great puffed and pearled sleeves rose to the pricked-eared pointings of the stiff lace about the head, conical and braided. The deep accumulation of dress fell about her in groined shadows, the train, rambling through a vista of primitive trees, was carpet-thick. She seemed to be expecting a bird. The gentleman was seated precariously on a charger. He seemed not so much to have mounted the animal, as to be about to descend upon him. The blue of an Italian sky lay between the saddle and the buff of the tightened rump of the rider. The charger had been caught by the painter in the execution of a falling arc, the mane lifted away in a dying swell; the tail forward and in, between thin bevelled legs. The gentleman's dress was a baffling mixture of the Romantic and the Religious, and in the cradling crook of his left arm he carried a plumed hat, crown out. The whole conception might have been a Mardi Gras whim. The gentleman's head, stuck on at a three-quarter angle, had a remarkable resemblance to Guido Volkbein, the same sweeping Cabalistic line of nose, the features seasoned and warm save where the virgin blue of the eyeballs curved out the lids as if another medium than that of sight had taken its stand beneath that flesh. There was no interval in the speed of that stare, endless and objective. The likeness was accidental. Had anyone cared to look into the matter they would have discovered these canvases to be reproductions of two intrepid and ancient actors. Guido had found them in some forgotten and dusty corner and had purchased them when he had been sure that he would need an alibi for the blood.

At this point exact history stopped for Felix who, thirty years later, turned up in the world with these facts, the two portraits and nothing more. His aunt, combing her long braids with an amber comb, told him what she knew, and this had been her only knowledge of his past. What had formed Felix from the date of his birth to his coming to thirty was unknown to the world, for the step of the wandering Jew is in every son. No matter where and when you meet him you feel that he has come from some place – no matter from what place he has come – some country that he has devoured rather than resided in, some secret land that he has been nourished on but cannot inherit, for the Jew seems to be everywhere from nowhere. When Felix's name was mentioned, three or more persons would swear to having seen him the week before in three different countries simultaneously.

Felix called himself Baron Volkbein, as his father had done before him. How Felix lived, how he came by his money – he knew figures as a dog knows the covey and as indefatigably he pointed and ran – how he mastered seven languages and served that knowledge well, no one knew. Many people were familiar with his figure and face. He was not popular, though the posthumous acclaim meted out to his father secured from his acquaintances the peculiar semicircular stare of those, who, unwilling to greet with earthly equality, nevertheless give to the living branch (because of death and its sanction) the slight bend of the head – a reminiscent pardon for future apprehension – a bow very common to us when in the presence of this people.

Felix was heavier than his father and taller. His hair began too far back on his forehead. His face was a long stout oval, suffering a laborious melancholy. One feature alone spoke of Hedvig, the mouth, which, though sensuous from lack of desire as hers had been from denial, pressed too intimately close to the bony structure of the teeth. The other features were a little heavy, the chin, the nose, and the lids; into one was set his monocle which shone, a round blind eye in the sun.

He was usually seen walking or driving alone, dressed as if expecting to participate in some great event, though there was no function in the world for which he could be said to be properly garbed; wishing to be correct at any moment, he was tailored in part for the evening and in part for the day.

From the mingled passions that made up his past, out of a diversity of bloods, from the crux of a thousand impossible situations, Felix had become the accumulated and single – the embarrassed.

His embarrassment took the form of an obsession for what he termed 'Old Europe': aristocracy, nobility, royalty. He spoke any given title with a pause before and after the name. Knowing circumlocution to be his only contact, he made it interminable and exacting. With the fury of a fanatic he hunted down his own disqualification, re-articulating the bones of the Imperial Courts long forgotten (those long remembered can alone claim to be long forgotten), listening with an unbecoming loquacity to officials and guardians for fear that his inattention might lose him some fragment of his resuscitation. He felt that the great past might mend a little if he bowed low enough, if he succumbed and gave homage.

In 1920 he was in Paris (his blind eye had kept him out of the army), still spatted, still wearing his cutaway, bowing, searching, with quick pendulous movements, for the correct thing to which to pay tribute: the right street, the right café, the right building, the right vista. In restaurants he bowed slightly to anyone who looked as if he might be 'someone', making the bend so imperceptible that the surprised person might think he was merely adjusting his stomach. His rooms were taken because a Bourbon had been carried from them to death. He kept a valet and a cook; the one because he looked like Louis the Fourteenth and the other because she resembled Queen Victoria, Victoria in another cheaper material, cut to the poor man's purse.

In his search for the particular *comédie humaine* Felix had come upon the odd. Conversant with edicts and laws, folk story and heresy, taster of rare wines, thumber of rarer books and old wives' tales – tales of men who became holy and of beasts that became damned – read in all plans for fortifications and bridges, given pause by all graveyards on all roads, a pedant of many churches and castles, his mind dimly and reverently reverberated to Madame de Sévigné, Goethe, Loyola and Brantôme. But Loyola sounded the deepest note, he was alone, apart and single. A race that has fled its generations from city to city has not found the necessary time for the accumulation of that toughness which produces ribaldry, nor, after the crucifixion of its ideas, enough forgetfulness in twenty centuries to create legend. It takes a Christian, standing eternally in the Jew's salvation, to blame himself and to bring up from that depth charming and fantastic superstitions through which the slowly and tirelessly milling Jew once more becomes the 'collector' of his own past. His undoing is never profitable until some *goy* has put it back into such shape that it can again be offered as a 'sign'. A Jew's undoing is never his own, it is God's; his rehabilitation is never his own, it is a Christian's. The Christian traffic in retribution has made the Jew's history a commodity; it is the medium through which he receives, at the necessary moment, the serum of his own past that he may offer it again as his blood. In this manner the Jew participates in the two conditions; and in like manner Felix took the breast of this wet nurse whose milk was his being but which could never be his birthright.

Early in life Felix had insinuated himself into the pageantry of the circus and the theatre. In some way they linked his emotions to the higher and unattainable pageantry of kings and queens. The more amiable actresses of Prague, Vienna, Hungary, Germany, France and Italy, the acrobats and sword-swallowers, had at one time or another allowed him their dressing rooms – sham salons in which he aped his heart. Here he had neither to be capable nor alien. He became for a little while a part of their splendid and reeking falsification.

The people of this world, with desires utterly divergent from his own, had also seized on titles for a purpose. There was a Princess Nadja, a Baron von Tink, a Principessa Stasera y Stasero, a King Buffo and a Duchess of Broadback: gaudy, cheap cuts from the beast life, immensely capable of that great disquiet called entertainment. They took titles merely to dazzle boys about town, to make their public life (and it was all they had) mysterious and perplexing, knowing well that skill is never so amazing as when it seems inappropriate. Felix clung to his title to dazzle his own estrangement. It brought them together.

Going among these people, the men smelling weaker and the women stronger than their beasts, Felix had that sense of peace that formerly he had experienced only in museums. He moved with a humble hysteria among the decaying brocades and laces of the Carnavalet; he loved that old and documented splendour with something of the love of the lion for its tamer – that sweat-tarnished spangled enigma that, in bringing the beast to heel, had somehow turned toward him a face like his own, but which though curious and weak, had yet picked the precise fury from his brain.

Nadja had sat back to Felix, as certain of the justice of his eye as she would have been of the linear justice of a Rops, knowing that Felix tabulated precisely the tense capability of her spine with its lashing curve swinging into the hard compact cleft of her rump, as angrily and as beautifully as the more obvious tail of her lion.

The emotional spiral of the circus, taking its flight from the immense disqualification of the public, rebounding from its illimitable hope, produced in Felix longing and disquiet. The circus was a loved thing that he could never touch, therefore never know. The people of the theatre and the ring were for him as dramatic and as monstrous as a consignment on which he could never bid. That he haunted them as persistently as he did, was evidence of something in his nature that was turning Christian.

He was, in like manner, amazed to find himself drawn to the church, though this tension he could handle with greater ease; its arena he found was circumscribed to the individual heart.

It was to the Duchess of Broadback (Frau Mann) that Felix owed his first audience with a 'gentleman of quality'. Frau Mann, then in Berlin, explained that this person had been 'somewhat mixed up with her in the past'. It was with the utmost difficulty that he could imagine her 'mixed up' with anyone, her coquetries were muscular and localized. Her trade – the trapeze – seemed to have preserved her. It gave her, in a way, a certain charm. Her legs had the specialized tension common to aerial workers; something of the bar was in her wrists, the tan bark in her walk, as if the air, by its very lightness, by its very non-resistance, were an almost insurmountable problem, making her body, though slight and compact, seem much heavier than that of women who stay upon the ground. In her face was the tense expression of an organism surviving in an alien element. She seemed to have a skin that was the pattern of her costume: a bodice of lozenges, red and yellow, low in the back and ruffled over and under the arms, faded with the reek of her three-a-day control, red tights, laced boots – one somehow felt they ran through her as the design runs through hard holiday candies, and the bulge in the groin where she took the bar, one foot caught in the flex of the calf, was as solid, specialized and as polished as oak. The stuff of the tights was no longer a covering, it was herself; the span of the tightly stitched crotch was so much her own flesh that she was as unsexed as a doll. The needle that had made one the property of the child made the other the property of no man.

'Tonight,' Frau Mann said turning to Felix, 'we are going to be amused. Berlin is sometimes very nice at night, *nicht wahr*? And the Count is something that must be seen. The place is very handsome, red and blue, he's fond of blue, God knows why, and he is fond of impossible people, so we are invited –' The Baron moved his foot in. 'He might even have the statues on.'

'Statues?' said Felix.

'The living statues,' she said, 'he simply adores them.' Felix dropped his hat; it rolled and stopped.

'Is he German?' he said.

'Oh no, Italian, but it does not matter, he speaks anything, I think he comes to Germany to change money – he comes, he goes away, and everything goes on the same, except that people have something to talk about.'

'What did you say his name was?'

'I didn't, but he calls himself Count Onatorio Altamonte,

I'm sure it's quite ridiculous, he says he is related to every nation – that should please you. We will have dinner, we will have champagne.' The way she said 'dinner' and the way she said 'champagne' gave meat and liquid their exact difference, as if by having surmounted two mediums, earth and air, her talent, running forward, achieved all others.

'Does one enjoy herself?' he asked.

'Oh, absolutely.'

She leaned forward, she began removing the paint with the hurried technical felicity of an artist cleaning a palette. She looked at the Baron derisively. '*Wir setzen an dieser Stelle über den Fluss –*' she said.

Standing about a table at the end of the immense room, looking as if they were deciding the fate of a nation, were grouped ten men, all in parliamentary attitudes, and one young woman. They were listening, at the moment of the entrance of Felix and the Duchess of Broadback, to a middle-aged 'medical student' with shaggy eyebrows, a terrific widow's peak, over-large dark eyes, and a heavy way of standing that was also apologetic. The man was Dr Matthew O'Connor, an Irishman from the Barbary Coast (Pacific Street, San Francisco), whose interest in gynaecology had driven him half around the world. He was taking the part of host, the Count not yet having made his appearance, and was telling of himself, for he considered himself the most amusing predicament.

'We may all be nature's noblemen,' he was saying, and the mention of a nobleman made Felix feel happier the instant he caught the word, though what followed left him in some doubt, 'but think of the stories that do not amount to much! That is, that are forgotten in spite of all man remembers (unless he remembers himself) merely because

13

they befell him without distinction of office or title – that's what we call legend and it's the best a poor man may do with his fate; the other,' he waved an arm, 'we call history, the best the high and mighty can do with theirs. Legend is unexpurgated, but history, because of its actors, is deflowered – every nation with a sense of humour is a lost nation, and every woman with a sense of humour is a lost woman. The Jews are the only people who have sense enough to keep humour in the family; a Christian scatters it all over the world.'

'*Ja! das ist ganz richtig* –' said the Duchess in a loud voice, but the interruption was quite useless. Once the doctor had his audience – and he got his audience by the simple device of pronouncing at the top of his voice (at such moments as irritable and possessive as a maddened woman's) some of the more boggish and biting of the shorter early Saxon verbs – nothing could stop him. He merely turned his large eyes upon her and having done so noticed her and her attire for the first time, which bringing suddenly to his mind something forgotten but comparable, sent him into a burst of laughter, exclaiming: 'Well, but God works in mysterious ways to bring things up in my mind! Now I am thinking of Nikka, the nigger who used to fight the bear in the Cirque de Paris. There he was, crouching all over the arena without a stitch on, except an ill-concealed loincloth all abulge as if with a deep sea catch, tattooed from head to heel with all the *ameublement* of depravity! Garlanded with rosebuds and hack-work of the devil – was he a sight to see! Though he couldn't have done a thing (and I know what I am talking about in spite of all that has been said about the black boys) if you had stood him in a gig-mill for a week, though (it's said) at a stretch it spelled Desdemona. Well then, over his belly was an angel from

Chartres, on each buttock, half public, half private, a quotation from the book of magic, a confirmation of the Jansenist theory, I'm sorry to say and here to say it. Across his knees, I give you my word, "I" on one and on the other, "can", put those together! Across his chest, beneath a beautiful caravel in full sail, two clasped hands, the wrist bones fretted with point lace. On each bosom an arrow-speared heart, each with different initials but with equal drops of blood; and running into the arm-pit, all down one side, the word said by Prince Arthur Tudor, son of King Henry the Seventh, when on his bridal night he called for a goblet of water (or was it water?). His Chamberlain, wondering at the cause of such drought, remarked on it and was answered in one word so wholly epigrammatic and in no way befitting the great and noble British Empire that he was brought up with a start, and that is all we will ever know of it, unless,' said the doctor, striking his hand on his hip, 'you are as good at guessing as Tiny M'Caffery.'

'And the legs?' Felix asked uncomfortably.

'The legs,' said Dr O'Connor, 'were devoted entirely to vine work, topped by the swart rambler rose copied from the coping of the Hamburg house of Rothschild. Over his *dos*, believe it or not and I shouldn't, a terse account in early monkish script – called by some people indecent, by others Gothic – of the really deplorable condition of Paris before hygiene was introduced, and nature had its way up to the knees. And just above what you mustn't mention, a bird flew carrying a streamer on which was incised, "*Garde tout!*" I asked him why all this barbarity; he answered he loved beauty and would have it about him.'

'Are you acquainted with Vienna?' Felix inquired.

'Vienna,' said the doctor, 'the bed into which the common people climb, docile with toil, and out of which the nobility fling themselves, ferocious with dignity – I do, but not so well but that I remember some of it still. I remember young Austrian boys going to school, flocks of quail they were, sitting out their recess in different spots in the sun, rosy-cheeked, bright-eyed, with damp rosy mouths, smelling of the herd childhood, facts of history glimmering in their minds like sunlight, soon to be lost, soon to be forgotten, degraded into proof. Youth is cause, effect is age; so with the thickening of the neck we get data.'

'I was not thinking of its young boys, but of its military superiority, its great names,' Felix said, feeling that the evening was already lost, seeing that as yet the host had not made his appearance and that no one seemed to know it or to care and that the whole affair was to be given over to this volatile person who called himself a doctor.

'The army, the celibate's family!' grinned the doctor. 'His one safety.'

The young woman, who was in her late twenties, turned from the group, coming closer to Felix and the doctor. She rested her hands behind her against the table. She seemed embarrassed. 'Are you both really saying what you mean, or are you just talking?' Having spoken, her face flushed, she added hurriedly, 'I am doing advance publicity for the circus, I'm Nora Flood.'

The doctor swung around, looking pleased. 'Ah!' he said. 'Nora suspects the cold incautious melody of time crawling, but,' he added, 'I've only just started.' Suddenly he struck his thigh with his open hand. 'Flood, Nora, why sweet God, my girl, I helped to bring you into the world!'

Felix, as disquieted as if he were expected to 'do something' to avert a catastrophe (as one is expected to do something about an overturned tumbler, the contents of which is about to drip over the edge of the table and into a lady's lap), on the phrase 'time crawling' broke into uncontrollable laughter, and though this occurrence troubled him the rest of his life he was never able to explain it to himself. The company, instead of being silenced, went on as if nothing had happened, two or three of the younger men were talking about something scandalous, and the 'Duchess' in her loud empty voice was telling a very stout man something about the living statues. This only added to the Baron's torment. He began waving his hands, saying, 'Oh, please! please!' and suddenly he had a notion that he was doing something that wasn't laughing at all, but something much worse, though he kept saying to himself, 'I am laughing, really laughing, nothing else whatsoever!' He kept waving his arms in distress and saying, 'Please, please!' staring at the floor, deeply embarrassed to find himself doing so.

As abruptly he sat straight up, his hands on the arms of the chair, staring fixedly at the doctor, who was leaning forward as he drew a chair up exactly facing him. 'Yes,' said the doctor, and he was smiling, 'you will be disappointed! *In questa tomba oscura* – oh, unfaithful one! I am no herbalist, I am no Rutebeuf, I have no panacea, I am not a mountebank – that is, I cannot or will not stand on my head. I'm no tumbler, neither a friar, nor yet a thirteenth-century Salome dancing arse up on a pair of Toledo blades – try to get any lovesick girl, male or female, to do that to-day! If you don't believe such things happened in the long back of yesterday look up the manuscripts in the British Museum or go to the Cathedral of Clermont-Ferrand, it's all one to me; become as the rich Mussulmans of Tunis who hire silly women to reduce the hour to its minimum of sense, still it will not be a cure, for there is none that takes place all at once in any man. You know what man really desires?' inquired the doctor, grinning into the immobile face of the Baron. 'One of two things: to find someone who is so stupid that he can lie to her, or to love someone so much that she can lie to him.'

'I was not thinking of women at all,' the Baron said, and he tried to stand up.

'Neither was I,' said the doctor, 'sit down.' He refilled his glass. 'The *fine* is very good,' he said.

Felix answered, 'No, thank you, I never drink.'

'You will,' the doctor said. 'Let us put it the other way, the Lutheran or Protestant church versus the Catholic. The Catholic is the girl that you love so much that she can lie to you, and the Protestant is the girl that loves you so much that you can lie to her, and pretend a lot that you do not feel. Luther, and I hope you don't mind my saying so, was as bawdy an old ram as ever trampled his own straw, because the custody of the people's 'remissions' of sins and indulgences had been snatched out of his hands, which was in that day in the shape of half of all they had and which the old monk of Wittenberg had intended to get off with in his own way. So, of course, after that, he went wild and chattered like a monkey in a tree and started something he never thought to start (or so the writing on his side of the breakfast table would seem to confirm), an obscene megalomania – and wild and wanton stranger that *that* is, it must come clear and cool and long or not at all. What do you listen to in the Protestant church? To the words of a man who has been chosen for his eloquence – and not too eloquent either, mark you, or he gets the bum's rush from the pulpit, for fear that in the end he will use his golden tongue for political ends. For a golden tongue is never satisfied until it has wagged itself over the destiny of a nation, and this the church is wise enough to know.

'But turn to the Catholic church, go into mass at any moment – what do you walk in upon? Something that's already in your blood. You know the story that the priest is telling as he moves from one side of the altar to the other, be he a cardinal, Leo X, or just some poor bastard from Sicily who has discovered that *pecca fortiter* among his goats no longer masses his soul, and has, God knows, been God's child from the start – it makes no difference. Why? Because you are sitting there with your own meditations *and* a legend (which is nipping the fruit as the wren bites), and mingling them both with the Holy Spoon, which is that story; or you can get yourself into the confessional, where, in sonorous prose, lacking contrition (if you must) you can speak of the condition of the knotty, tangled soul and be answered in Gothic echoes, mutual and instantaneous – one saying hail to your farewell. Mischief unravels and the fine high hand of heaven proffers the skein again, combed and forgiven!'

'The one House,' he went on, 'is hard, as hard as the gift of gab, and the other is as soft as a goat's hip, and you can blame no man for anything, and you can't like them at all.'

'Wait!' said Felix.

'Yes?' said the doctor.

Felix bending forward, deprecatory and annoyed, went on: 'I like the prince who was reading a book, when the executioner touched him on the shoulder telling him that it was time, and he, arising, laid a paper-cutter between the pages to keep his place and closed the book.'

'Ah,' said the doctor, 'that is not man living in his moment, it is man living in his miracle.' He refilled his glass. '*Gesundheit*,' he said; '*Freude sei Euch von Gott beschieden, wie heut' so immerdar!*'

'You argue about sorrow and confusion too easily,' Nora said.

'Wait!' the doctor answered. 'A man's sorrow runs uphill; true it is difficult for him to bear, but it is also difficult for him to keep. I, as a medical man, know in what pocket a man keeps his heart and soul, and in what jostle of the liver, kidneys and genitalia these pockets are pilfered. There is no pure sorrow. Why? It is bedfellow to lungs, lights, bones, guts and gall! There are only confusions, about that you are quite right, Nora my child, confusions and defeated anxieties – there you have us, one and all. If you are a gymnosophist you *can* do without clothes, and if you are gimp-legged you will know more wind between the knees than another, still it is confusion; God's chosen walk close to the wall.'

'I was in the war once myself,' the doctor went on, 'in a little town where the bombs began tearing the heart out of you, so that you began to think of all the majesty in the world that you would not be able to think of in a minute, if the noise came down and struck in the right place; I was scrambling for the cellar – and in it was an old Breton woman and a cow she had dragged with her, and behind that someone from Dublin, saying, "Glory be to God!" in a whisper at the far end of the animal. Thanks be to my Maker, I had her head on, and the poor beast trembling on her four legs so I knew all at once that the tragedy of the beast can be two legs more awful than a man's. She was softly dropping her dung at the far end where the thin Celtic voice kept coming up saying, "Glory be to Jesus!" and I said to myself, "Can't the morning come now, so I can see what my face is mixed up with?" At that a flash of lightning went by and I saw the cow turning her head straight back so her horns made two moons against her shoulders, the tears soused all over her great black eyes.

'I began talking to her, cursing myself and the mick, and

the old woman looking as if she were looking down her life, sighting it the way a man looks down the barrel of a gun for an aim. I put my hand on the poor bitch of a cow and her hide was running water under my hand, like water tumbling down from Lahore, jerking against my hand as if she wanted to go, standing still in one spot; and I thought, there are directions and speeds that no one has calculated, for believe it or not that cow had gone somewhere very fast that we didn't know of, and yet was still standing there.'

The doctor lifted the bottle. 'Thank you,' said Felix, 'I never drink spirits.'

'You will,' said the doctor.

'There's one thing that has always troubled me,' the doctor continued, 'this matter of the guillotine. They say that the headsman has to supply his own knife, as a husband is supposed to supply his own razor. That's enough to rot his heart out before he has whittled one head. Wandering about the Boul "Mich" one night, flittering my eyes, I saw one with a red carnation in his buttonhole. I asked him what he was wearing it for, just to start up a friendly conversation, he said, "It's the headsman's pre-rogative," – and I went as limp as a blotter snatched from the Senate. "At one time," he said, "the executioner gripped it between his teeth," at that my bowels turned turtle, seeing him in my mind's eye stropping the cleaver with a bloom in his mouth, like Carmen, and he the one man who is supposed to keep his gloves on in church! They often end by slicing themselves up, it's a rhythm that finally meets their own neck. He leaned forward and drew a finger across mine and said, "As much hair as thick as that makes it a little difficult," and at that moment I got heart failure for the rest of my life. I put down a franc and flew like the wind, the hair on my back standing as high as Queen

Anne's ruff! And I didn't stop until I found myself spang in the middle of the Musée de Cluny, clutching the rack.'

A sudden silence went over the room. The Count was standing in the doorway, rocking on his heels, either hand on the sides of the door, a torrent of Italian, which was merely the culmination of some theme he had begun in the entrance hall, was abruptly halved as he slapped his leg, standing tall and bent and peering. He moved forward into the room, holding with thumb and forefinger the centre of a round magnifying glass which hung from a broad black ribbon. With the other hand he moved from chair to table, from guest to guest. Behind him, in a riding habit, was a young girl. Having reached the sideboard he swung around with gruesome nimbleness.

'Get out!' he said softly, laying his hand on the girl's shoulder. 'Get out, get out!' It was obvious he meant it; he bowed slightly.

As they reached the street the 'Duchess' caught a swirling hem of lace about her chilling ankles. 'Well, my poor devil?' she said, turning to Felix.

'Well!' said Felix. 'What was that about, and why?'

The doctor hailed a cab with the waving end of a bulldog cane. 'That can be repaired at any bar,' he said.

'The name of that,' said the Duchess, pulling on her gloves, 'is a brief audience with the great, brief, but an audience!'

As they went up the darkened street Felix felt himself turning scarlet. 'Is he really a Count?' he asked.

'*Herr Gott!*' said the Duchess. 'Am I what I say? Are you? Is the doctor?' She put her hand on his knee. 'Yes or no?'

The doctor was lighting a cigarette and in its flare the Baron saw that he was grinning. 'He put us out for one of those hopes that is about to be defeated.' He waved his gloves from the window to other guests who were standing along the kerb, hailing vehicles.

'What do you mean?' the Baron said in a whisper.

'Count Onatorio Altamonte – may the name eventually roll over the Ponte Vecchio and into the Arno – suspected that he had come upon his last erection.'

The doctor began to sing, '*Nur eine Nacht.*'

Frau Mann, with her face pressed against the cab window, said, 'It's snowing.' At her words Felix turned his coat collar up.

'Where are we going?' he asked Frau Mann. She was quite gay again.

'Let us go to Heinrich's, I always do when it's snowing. He mixes the drinks stronger then, and he's a good customer, he always takes in the show.'

'Very well,' said the doctor, preparing to rap on the window. 'Where is thy Heinrich?'

'Go down Unter den Linden,' Frau Mann said. 'I'll tell you when.'

Felix said, 'If you don't mind, I'll get down here.' He got down, walking against the snow.

Seated in the warmth of the favoured café, the doctor, unwinding his scarf said: 'There's something missing and whole about the Baron Felix – damned from the waist up, which reminds me of Mademoiselle Basquette who was damned from the waist down, a girl without legs, built like a medieval abuse. She used to wheel herself through the Pyrenees on a board. What there was of her was beautiful in a cheap traditional sort of way, the face that one sees on people who come to a racial, not a personal, amazement. I wanted to give her a present for what of her was missing, and she said, "Pearls – they go so well with everything!" Imagine, and the other half of her still in God's bag of

23

tricks! Don't tell me that what was missing had not taught her the value of what was present. Well, in any case,' the doctor went on rolling down his gloves, 'a sailor saw her one day and fell in love with her. She was going uphill and the sun was shining all over her back, it made a saddle across her bent neck and flickered along the curls of her head, gorgeous and bereft as the figure head of a Norse vessel that the ship has abandoned. So he snatched her up, board and all, and took her away and had his will; when he got good and tired of her, just for gallantry, he put her down on her board about five miles out of town, so she had to roll herself back again, weeping something fearful to see, because one is accustomed to see tears falling down to the feet. Ah truly, a pine board may come up to the chin of a woman and still she will find reason to weep. I tell you Madame, if one gave birth to a heart on a plate, it would say "Love" and twitch like the lopped leg of a frog.'

'*Wunderbar!*' exclaimed Frau Mann. '*Wunderbar*, my God!'

'I'm not through,' said the doctor, laying his gloves across his knees, 'someday I am going to see the Baron again, and when I do I shall tell him about the mad Wittelsbach. He'll look as distressed as an owl tied up in a muffler.'

'Ah,' exclaimed Frau Mann, 'he will enjoy it. He is so fond of titles.'

'Listen,' the doctor said, ordering a round, 'I don't want to talk of the Wittelsbach. Oh God, when I think back to my past, everyone in my family a beauty, my mother, with hair on her head as red as a fire kicked over in spring (and that was early in the eighties when a girl was the toast of the town, and going the limit meant lobster à la Newburg). She had a hat on her as big as the top of a table, and everything on it but running water; her bosom clinched into a corset of

24

buckram, and my father sitting up beside her (snapped while they were riding on a roller-coaster). He had on one of those silly little yellow jackets and a tan bowler just up over his ears, and he must have been crazy, for he was sort of cross-eyed – maybe it was the wind in his face or thoughts of my mother where he couldn't do anything about it.' Frau Mann took up her glass, looking at it with one eye closed – 'I've an album of my own,' she said in a warm voice, 'and everyone in it looks like a soldier – even though they are dead.'

The doctor grinned, biting his teeth. Frau Mann tried to light a cigarette, the match wavered from side to side in her unsteady hand.

Frau Mann was slightly tipsy, and the insistent hum of the doctor's words was making her sleepy.

Seeing that Frau Mann dozed, the doctor got up lightly and tiptoed noiselessly to the entrance. He said to the waiter in bad German: 'The lady will pay,' opened the door, and went quietly into the night.

CHAPTER TWO

La Somnambule

Close to the church of St Sulpice, around the corner in the
rue Servandoni, lived the doctor. His small slouching figure
was a feature of the Place. To the proprietor of the Café de
la Mairie du VIe he was almost a son. This relatively small
square, through which tram lines ran in several directions,
bounded on the one side by the church and on the other by
the court, was the doctor's 'city'. What he could not find
here to answer to his needs, could be found in the narrow
streets that ran into it. Here he had been seen ordering
details for funerals in the parlour with its black broadcloth
curtains and mounted pictures of hearses; buying holy
pictures and *petits Jésus* in the boutique displaying
vestments and flowering candles. He had shouted down at
least one judge in the Mairie du Luxembourg after a dozen
cigars had failed to bring about his ends.

He walked, pathetic and alone, among the pasteboard
booths of the Foire St Germain when for a time its imitation
castles squatted in the square. He was seen coming at a
smart pace down the left side of the church to go into Mass;
bathing in the holy water stoup as if he were its single and
beholden bird, pushing aside weary French maids and local
tradespeople with the impatience of a soul in physical
stress.

Sometimes, late at night, before turning into the Café de la Mairie de VIe, he would be observed staring up at the huge towers of the church which rose into the sky, unlovely but reassuring, running a thick warm finger around his throat, where, in spite of its custom, his hair surprised him, lifting along his back and creeping up over his collar. Standing small and insubordinate, he would watch the basins of the fountain loosing their skirts of water in a ragged and flowing hem, sometimes crying to a man's departing shadow: 'Aren't you the beauty!'

To the Café de la Mairie du VIe he brought Felix, who turned up in Paris some weeks after the encounter in Berlin. Felix thought to himself that undoubtedly the doctor was a great liar, but a valuable liar. His fabrications seemed to be the framework of a forgotten but imposing plan; some condition of life of which he was the sole surviving retainer. His manner was that of a servant of a defunct noble family, whose movements recall, though in a degraded form, those of a late master. Even the doctor's favourite gesture – plucking hairs out of his nostrils – seemed the 'vulgarization' of what was once a thoughtful plucking of the beard.

As the altar of a church would present but a barren stylization but for the uncalculated offerings of the confused and humble; as the corsage of a woman is made suddenly martial and sorrowful by the rose thrust among the more decorous blooms by the hand of a lover suffering the violence of the overlapping of the permission to bestow a last embrace, and its withdrawal: making a vanishing and infinitesimal bull's eye of that which had a moment before been a buoyant and showy bosom, by dragging time out of his bowels (for a lover knows two times, that which he is given, and that which he must make) – so Felix was astonished to find that the most touching flowers laid on

27

the altar he had raised to his imagination were placed there by the people of the underworld, and that the reddest was to be the rose of the doctor.

After a long silence in which the doctor had ordered and consumed a *Chambéry fraise* and the Baron a coffee, the doctor remarked that the Jew and the Irish, the one moving upward and the other down, often meet, spade to spade in the same acre.

'The Irish may be as common as whale-shit – excuse me – on the bottom of the ocean – forgive me – but they do have imagination and,' he added, 'creative misery, which comes from being smacked down by the devil, and lifted up again by the angels. *Misericordioso!* Save me, Mother Mary, and never mind the other fellow! But the Jew, what is he at his best? Never anything higher than a meddler – pardon my wet glove – a supreme and marvellous meddler often, but a meddler nevertheless.' He bowed slightly from the hips. 'All right, Jews meddle and we lie, that's the difference, the fine difference. We say someone is pretty for instance, whereas, if the truth were known, they are probably as ugly as Smith going backward, but by our lie we have made that very party powerful, such is the power of the charlatan, the great strong! They drop on anything at any moment, and that sort of thing makes the mystic in the end, and,' he added, 'it makes the great doctor. The only people who really *know* anything about medical science are the nurses, and they never tell, they'd get slapped if they did. But the great doctor, he's a divine idiot and a wise man. He closes one eye, the eye that he studied with, and putting his fingers on the arteries of the body says: "God, whose roadway this is, has given me permission to travel on it also," which, heaven help the patient, is true; in this manner he comes on great cures, and sometimes upon that road is disconcerted by that

Little Man.' The doctor ordered another *Chambéry*, and asked the Baron what he would have; being told that he wished nothing for the moment, the doctor added: 'No man needs curing of his individual sickness, his universal malady is what he should look to.'

The Baron remarked that this sounded like dogma.

The doctor grinned. 'Does it? Well, when you see that Little Man you know you will be shouldered from the path.'

'I also know this,' he went on: 'One cup poured into another makes different water; tears shed by one eye would blind if wept into another's eye. The breast we strike in joy is not the breast we strike in pain; any man's smile would be consternation on another's mouth. Rear up eternal river, here comes grief! Man has no foothold that is not also a bargain. So be it! Laughing I came into Pacific Street, and laughing I'm going out of it; laughter is the pauper's money. I like paupers and bums,' he added, 'because they are impersonal with misery, but me – me, I'm taken most and chiefly for a vexatious bastard and gum on the bow, the wax that clots the gall or middle blood of man known at the heart or Bundle of Hiss. May my dilator burst and my speculum rust, may panic seize my index finger before I point out my man.'

His hands (which he always carried like a dog who is walking on his hind legs) seemed to be holding his attention, then he said, raising his large melancholy eyes with the bright twinkle that often came into them: 'Why is it that whenever I hear music I think I'm a bride?'

'Neurasthenia,' said Felix.

He shook his head. 'No, I'm not neurasthenic, I haven't that much respect for people – the basis, by the way, of all neurasthenia.'

'Impatience.'

The doctor nodded. 'The Irish are impatient for eternity, they lie to hurry it up, and they maintain their balance by the dexterity of God, God and the Father.'

'In 1685,' the Baron said, with dry humour, 'the Turks brought coffee into Vienna, and from that day Vienna, like a woman, had one impatience, something she liked. You know, of course, that Pitt the younger was refused alliance because he was foolish enough to proffer tea; Austria and tea could never go together. All cities have a particular and special beverage suited to them. As for God and the Father – in Austria they were the Emperor.' The doctor looked up. The *chasseur* of the Hôtel Récamier (whom he knew far too well) was approaching them at a run.

'Eh!' said the doctor, who always expected anything at any hour, 'Now what?' The boy, standing before him in a red and black striped vest and flapping soiled apron, exclaimed in Midi French that a lady in twenty-nine had fainted and could not be brought out of it.

The doctor got up slowly, sighing. 'Pay,' he said to Felix, 'and follow me.' None of the doctor's methods being orthodox, Felix was not surprised at the invitation, but did as he was told.

On the second landing of the hotel (it was one of those middle-class hostelries which can be found in almost any corner of Paris, neither good nor bad, but so typical that it might have been moved every night and not have been out of place) a door was standing open, exposing a red carpeted floor, and at the further end two narrow windows overlooking the square.

On a bed, surrounded by a confusion of potted plants, exotic palms and cut flowers, faintly oversung by the notes of unseen birds, which seemed to have been forgotten – left without the usual silencing cover, which, like cloaks on funeral urns, are cast over their cages at night by good housewives – half flung off the support of the cushions from which, in a moment of threatened consciousness she had turned her head, lay the young woman, heavy and dishevelled. Her legs, in white flannel trousers, were spread as in a dance, the thick lacquered pumps looking too lively for the arrested step. Her hands, long and beautiful, lay on either side of her face.

The perfume that her body exhaled was of the quality of that earth-flesh, fungi, which smells of captured dampness and yet is so dry, overcast with the odour of oil of amber, which is an inner malady of the sea, making her seem as if she had invaded a sleep incautious and entire. Her flesh was the texture of plant life, and beneath it one sensed a frame, broad, porous and sleep-worn, as if sleep were a decay fishing her beneath the visible surface. About her head there was an effulgence as of phosphorus glowing about the circumference of a body of water – as if her life lay through her in ungainly luminous deteriorations – the troubling structure of the born somnambule, who lives in two worlds – meet of child and desperado.

Like a painting by the *douanier* Rousseau, she seemed to lie in a jungle trapped in a drawing room (in the apprehension of which the walls have made their escape), thrown in among the carnivorous flowers as their ration; the set, the property of an unseen *dompteur*, half lord, half promoter, over which one expects to hear the strains of an orchestra of wood-wind render a serenade which will popularize the wilderness.

Felix, out of delicacy, stepped behind the palms. The doctor with professional roughness, brought to a pitch by his eternal fear of meeting with the Law (he was not a licensed practitioner) said: 'Slap her wrists, for Christ's sake. Where in hell is the water pitcher!'

He found it, and with amiable heartiness flung a handful against her face.

A series of almost invisible shudders wrinkled her skin as the water dripped from her lashes, over her mouth and on to the bed. A spasm of waking moved upward from some deep shocked realm, and she opened her eyes. Instantly she tried to get to her feet. She said: 'I was all right;' and fell back into the pose of her annihilation.

Experiencing a double confusion, Felix now saw the doctor partially hidden by the screen beside the bed, make the movements common to the 'dumbfounder', or man of magic; the gestures of one who, in preparing the audience for a miracle, must pretend that there is nothing to hide; the whole purpose that of making the back and elbows move in a series of 'honesties', while in reality the most flagrant part of the hoax is being prepared.

Felix saw that this was for the purpose of snatching a few drops from a perfume bottle picked up from the night table; of dusting his darkly bristled chin with a puff, and drawing a line of rouge across his lips, his upper lip compressed on his lower, in order to have it seem that their sudden embellishment was a visitation of nature; still thinking himself unobserved, as if the whole fabric of magic had begun to decompose, as if the mechanics of machination were indeed out of control and were simplifying themselves back to their origin; the doctor's hand reached out and covered a loose hundred franc note lying on the table.

With a tension in his stomach, such as one suffers when watching an acrobat leaving the virtuosity of his safety in a mad unravelling whirl into probable death, Felix watched the hand descend, take up the note, and disappear into the limbo of the doctor's pocket. He knew that he would continue to like the doctor, though he was aware that it would be in spite of a long series of convulsions of the spirit, analogous to the displacement in the fluids of the oyster, that must cover its itch with a pearl; so he would have to cover the doctor. He knew at the same time that this stricture of acceptance (by which what we must love is made into what we can love) would eventually be a part of himself, though originally brought on by no will of his own.

Engrossed in the coils of this new disquiet, Felix turned about. The girl was sitting up. She recognized the doctor. She had seen him somewhere. But, as one may trade ten years at a certain shop and be unable to place the shopkeeper if he is met in the street or in the *promenoir* of a theatre, the shop being a portion of his identity, she struggled to place him now that he had moved out of his frame.

'Café de la Mairie du VIe,' said the doctor, taking a chance in order to have a hand in her awakening.

She did not smile, though the moment he spoke she placed him. She closed her eyes and Felix, who had been looking into them intently because of their mysterious and shocking blue, found himself seeing them still faintly clear and timeless behind the lids – the long unqualified range in the iris of wild beasts who have not tamed the focus down to meet the human eye.

The woman who presents herself to the spectator as a 'picture' forever arranged, is, for the contemplative mind, the chiefest danger. Sometimes one meets a woman who is beast turning human. Such a person's every movement will reduce to an image of a forgotten experience; a mirage of an eternal wedding cast on the racial memory; as insupportable a joy as would be the vision of an eland coming down an aisle of trees, chapleted with orange blossoms and bridal veil, a hoof raised in the economy of fear, stepping in the trepidation of flesh that will become myth; as the unicorn is neither man nor beast deprived, but human hunger pressing its breast to its prey.

Such a woman is the infected carrier of the past: before her the structure of our head and jaws ache – we feel that we could eat her, she who is eaten death returning, for only then do we put our face close to the blood on the lips of our forefathers.

Something of this emotion came over Felix, but being racially incapable of abandon, he felt that he was looking upon a figurehead in a museum, which though static, no longer roosting on its cutwater, seemed yet to be going against the wind; as if this girl were the converging halves of a broken fate, setting face, in sleep, toward itself in time, as an image and its reflection in a lake seem parted only by the hesitation in the hour.

In the tones of this girl's voice was the pitch of one enchanted with the gift of postponed abandon: the low drawling 'aside' voice of the actor who, in the soft usury of his speech, withholds a vocabulary until the profitable moment when he shall be facing his audience – in her case a guarded extempore to the body of what would be said at some later period when she would be able to 'see' them. What she now said was merely the longest way to a quick dismissal. She asked them to come to see her when she would be 'able to feel better'.

Pinching the *chasseur*, the doctor inquired the girl's name. 'Mademoiselle Robin Vote,' the *chasseur* answered.

Descending into the street, the doctor, desiring 'one last before bed' directed his steps back to the café. After a short silence he asked the Baron if he had ever thought about women and marriage. He kept his eyes fixed on the marble

34

of the table before him, knowing that Felix had experienced something unusual.

The Baron admitted that he had, he wished a son who would feel as he felt about the 'great past'. The doctor then inquired, with feigned indifference, of what nation he would choose the boy's mother.

'The American,' the Baron answered instantly. 'With an American anything can be done.'

The doctor laughed. He brought his soft fist down on the table – now he was sure. 'Fate and entanglement,' he said, 'have begun again – the dung beetle rolling his burden uphill – oh the hard climb! Nobility, very well, but what is it?' The Baron started to answer him, the doctor held up his hand. 'Wait a minute! I know – the few that the many have lied about well and long enough to make them deathless. So you must have a son,' he paused. 'A king is the peasant's actor, who becomes so scandalous that he has to be bowed down to – scandalous in the higher sense naturally. And why must he be bowed down to? Because he has been set apart as the one dog who need not regard the rules of the house, they are so high that they can defame God and foul their rafters! But the people – that's different – they are church-broken, nation-broken – they drink and pray and piss in the one place. Every man has a house-broken heart except the great man. The people love their church and know it, as a dog knows where he was made to conform, and there he returns by his instinct. But to the graver permission, the king, the tsar, the emperor, who may relieve themselves on high heaven – to them they bow down – only.' The Baron, who was always troubled by obscenity, would never, in the case of the doctor, resent it; he felt the seriousness, the melancholy hidden beneath every jest and malediction that the doctor uttered, therefore he answered

35

him seriously. 'To pay homage to our past is the only gesture that also includes the future.'

'And so a son?'

'For that reason. The modern child has nothing left to hold to, or to put it better, he has nothing to hold with. We are adhering to life now with our last muscle – the heart.'

'The last muscle of aristocracy is madness – remember that –' the doctor leaned forward, 'the last child born to aristocracy is sometimes an idiot, out of respect – we go up – but we come down.'

The Baron dropped his monocle, the unarmed eye looked straight ahead. 'It's not necessary,' he said, then he added, 'But you are American, so you don't believe.'

'Ho!' hooted the doctor, 'because I'm American I believe anything, so I say beware! In the king's bed is always found, just before it becomes a museum piece, the droppings of the black sheep' – he raised his glass, 'To Robin Vote.' He grinned. 'She can't be more than twenty.'

With a roar the steel blind came down over the window of the Café de la Mairie du VIe.

Felix, carrying two volumes on the life of the Bourbons, called the next day at the Hôtel Récamier. Miss Vote was not in. Four afternoons in succession he called, only to be told that she had just left. On the fifth, turning the corner of the rue Bonaparte, he ran into her.

Removed from her setting – the plants that had surrounded her, the melancholy red velvet of the chairs and the curtains, the sound, weak and nocturnal, of the birds – she yet carried the quality of the 'way back' as animals do. She suggested that they should walk together in the gardens of the Luxembourg, toward which her steps had been directed when he addressed her. They walked in the bare chilly gardens and Felix was happy. He felt that he could talk to her, tell her anything, though she herself was so silent. He told her he had a post in the Crédit Lyonnais, earning two thousand five hundred francs a week; a master of seven tongues, he was useful to the bank, and, he added, he had a trifle saved up, gained in speculations.

He walked a little short of her. Her movements were slightly headlong and sideways; slow, clumsy and yet graceful, the ample gait of the nightwatch. She wore no hat, and her pale head, with its short hair growing flat on the forehead made still narrower by the hanging curls almost on a level with the finely arched eyebrows, gave her the look of cherubs in renaissance theatres; the eyeballs showing slightly rounded in profile, the temples low and square. She was gracious and yet fading, like an old statue in a garden, that symbolizes the weather through which it has endured, and is not so much the work of man as the work of wind and rain and the herd of the seasons, and though formed in man's image is a figure of doom. Because of this, Felix found her presence painful, and yet a happiness. Thinking of her, visualizing her, was an extreme act of the will; to recall her after she had gone, however, was as easy as the recollection of a sensation of beauty, without its details. When she smiled the smile was only in the mouth, and a little bitter: the face of an incurable yet to be stricken with its malady.

As the days passed they spent many hours in museums, and while this pleased Felix immeasurably, he was surprised that often her taste, turning from an appreciation of the most beautiful, would also include the cheaper and debased, with an emotion as real. When she touched a thing, her hands seemed to take the place of the eye. He thought: 'She has the touch of the blind who, because they see more with their fingers, forget more in their minds.' Her fingers would go forward, hesitate, tremble, as if they had found a face in the dark. When her hand finally came to rest, the palm closed, it was as if she had stopped a crying mouth. Her hand lay still and she would turn away. At such moments Felix experienced an unaccountable apprehension. The sensuality in her hands frightened him.

Her clothes were of a period that he could not quite place. She wore feathers of the kind his mother had worn, flattened sharply to the face. Her skirts were moulded to her hips and fell downward and out, wider and longer than those of other women, heavy silks that made her seem newly ancient. One day he learned the secret. Pricing a small tapestry in an antique shop facing the Seine, he saw Robin reflected in a door mirror of a back room, dressed in a heavy brocaded gown which time had stained in places, in others split, yet which was so voluminous that there were yards enough to refashion.

He found that his love for Robin was not in truth a selection; it was as if the weight of his life had amassed one precipitation. He had thought of making a destiny for himself, through laborious and untiring travail. Then with Robin it seemed to stand before him, without effort. When he asked her to marry him it was with such an unplanned eagerness that he was taken aback to find himself accepted as if Robin's life held no volition for refusal.

He took her first to Vienna. To reassure himself he showed her all the historic buildings. He kept saying to himself that sooner or later, in this garden or that palace, she would suddenly be moved as he was moved. Yet it seemed to him that he too was a sightseer. He tried to explain to her what Vienna had been before the war; what it must have been before he was born; yet his memory was confused and hazy, and he found himself repeating what he had read, for it was what he knew best. With methodic anxiety he took her over the city. He said, 'You are a *Baronin* now.' He spoke to her in German as she ate the heavy *Schnitzel* and dumplings, clasping her hand about the thick handle of the beer mug. He said: '*Das Leben ist ewig, darin liegt seine Schönheit.*'

They walked before the Imperial Palace in a fine hot sun that fell about the clipped hedges and the statues warm and clear. He went into the Kammergarten with her and talked, and on into the Gloriette, and sat on first one bench, and then another. Brought up short, he realized that he had been hurrying from one to the other as if they were orchestra chairs, as if he himself were trying not to miss anything; now, at the extremity of the garden, he was aware that he had been anxious to see every tree, every statue at a different angle.

In their hotel, she went to the window and pulled aside the heavy velvet hangings, threw down the bolster that Vienna uses against the wind at the ledge, and opened the window, though the night air was cold. He began speaking of Emperor Francis Joseph and of the whereabouts of Charles the First. And as he spoke, Felix laboured under the weight of his own remorseless re-creation of the great, generals and statesmen and emperors. His chest was as heavy as if it were supporting the combined weight of their apparel and their destiny. Looking up after an interminable flow of fact and fancy, he saw Robin sitting with her legs thrust out, her head thrown back against the embossed cushion of the chair, sleeping, one arm fallen over the chair's side, the hand somehow older and wiser than her body; and looking at her he knew that he was not sufficient to make her what he had hoped; it would require more than his own argument. It would require contact with persons exonerated of their earthly condition by some strong spiritual bias, someone of that old régime, some old lady of the past courts, who only remembered others when trying to think of herself.

On the tenth day, therefore, Felix turned about and re-entered Paris. In the following months he put his faith in the fact that Robin had Christian proclivities, and his hope in the discovery that she was an enigma. He said to himself that possibly she had greatness hidden in the noncommittal. He felt that her attention, somehow in spite of him, had already been taken, by something not yet in history. Always she seemed to be listening to the echo of some foray in the blood, that had no known setting; and when he came to know her this was all he could base his intimacy upon. There was something pathetic in the spectacle: Felix reiterating the tragedy of his father. Attired like some haphazard in the mind of a tailor, again in the ambit of his father's futile attempt to encompass the rhythm of his wife's stride, Felix, with tightly held monocle, walked beside Robin, talking to her, drawing her attention to this and that, wrecking himself and his peace of mind in an effort to acquaint her with the destiny for which he had chosen her; that she might bear sons who would recognize and honour the past. For without such love, the past as he understood it, would die away from the world. She was not listening and he said in an angry mood, though he said it calmly, 'I am deceiving you!' And he wondered what he meant, and why she did not hear.

'A child,' he pondered. 'Yes, a child!' and then he said to himself, 'Why has it not come about?' The thought took him abruptly in the middle of his accounting. He hurried home in a flurry of anxiety, as a boy who has heard a regiment on parade, toward which he cannot run because he has no one from whom to seek permission, and yet runs haltingly nevertheless. Coming face to face with her, all that he could stammer out was: 'Why is there no child? *Wo ist das Kind? Warum? Warum?*'

Robin prepared herself for her child with her only power: a stubborn cataleptic calm, conceiving herself pregnant before she was; and, strangely aware of some lost land in herself, she took to going out; wandering the countryside; to train travel, to other cities, alone and engrossed. Once, not having returned for three days, and Felix nearly beside himself with terror, she walked in late at night and said that she had been half-way to Berlin.

Suddenly she took the Catholic vow. She came into the church silently. The prayers of the suppliants had not ceased nor had anyone been broken of their meditation. Then, as if some inscrutable wish for salvation, something yet more monstrously unfulfilled than they had suffered, had thrown a shadow, they regarded her, to see her going softly forward and down, a tall girl with the body of a boy.

Many churches saw her: St Julien le Pauvre, the church of St Germain des Prés, Ste Clothilde. Even on the cold tiles of the Russian church, in which there is no pew, she knelt alone, lost and conspicuous, her broad shoulders above her neighbours, her feet large and as earthly as the feet of a monk.

She strayed into the rue Picpus, into the gardens of the convent of L'Adoration Perpétuelle. She talked to the nuns and they, feeling that they were looking at someone who would never be able to ask for, or receive, mercy, blessed her in their hearts and gave her a sprig of rose from the bush. They showed her where Jean Valjean had kept his rakes, and where the bright little ladies of the *pension* came to quilt their covers; and Robin smiled, taking the spray, and looked down at the tomb of Lafayette and thought her unpeopled thoughts. Kneeling in the chapel, which was never without a nun going over her beads, Robin, trying to bring her mind to this abrupt necessity, found herself worrying about her height. Was she still growing?

She tried to think of the consequence to which her son was to be born and dedicated. She thought of the Emperor Francis Joseph. There was something commensurate in the heavy body with the weight in her mind, where reason was inexact with lack of necessity. She wandered to thoughts of women, women that she had come to connect with women. Strangely enough these were women in history, Louise de la Vallière, Catherine of Russia, Madame de Maintenon, Catherine de Medici, and two women out of literature, Anna Karenina and Catherine Heathcliff; and now there was this woman Austria. She prayed, and her prayer was monstrous, because in it there was no margin left for damnation or forgiveness, for praise or for blame – those who cannot conceive a bargain cannot be saved or damned. She could not offer herself up; she only told of herself, in a preoccupation that was its own predicament.

Leaning her childish face and full chin on the shelf of the prie-Dieu, her eyes fixed, she laughed, out of some hidden capacity, some lost subterranean humour; as it ceased, she leaned still further forward in a swoon, waking and yet heavy, like one in sleep.

When Felix returned that evening Robin was dozing in a chair, one hand under her cheek and one arm fallen. A book was lying on the floor beneath her hand. The book was the memoirs of the Marquis de Sade; a line was underscored: *Et lui rendit pendant sa captivité les milles services qu'un amour dévoué est seul capable de rendre*, and suddenly into his mind came the question: 'What is wrong?'

She awoke but did not move. He came and took her by the arm and lifted her toward him. She put her hand against his chest and pushed him, she looked frightened, she opened her mouth but no words came. He stepped back, he tried to speak but they moved aside from each other saying nothing.

That night she was taken with pains. She began to curse loudly, a thing that Felix was totally unprepared for; with the most foolish gestures he tried to make her comfortable.

'Go to hell!' she cried. She moved slowly, bent away from him, chair by chair; she was drunk – her hair was swinging in her eyes.

Amid loud and frantic cries of affirmation and despair Robin was delivered. Shuddering in the double pains of birth and fury, cursing like a sailor, she rose up on her elbow in her bloody gown, looking about her in the bed as if she had lost something. 'Oh, for Christ's sake, for Christ's sake!' she kept crying like a child who has walked into the commencement of a horror.

A week out of bed she was lost, as if she had done something irreparable, as if this act had caught her attention for the first time.

One night, Felix, having come in unheard, found her standing in the centre of the floor holding the child high in her hand as if she were about to dash it down; but she brought it down gently.

The child was small, a boy, and sad. It slept too much in a quivering palsy of nerves, it made few voluntary movements; it whimpered.

Robin took to wandering again, to intermittent travel from which she came back hours, days later, disinterested. People were uneasy when she spoke to them; confronted with a catastrophe that had yet no beginning.

Felix had each day the sorrow born with him; for the rest, he pretended that he noticed nothing. Robin was almost never home; he did not know how to inquire for her. Sometimes coming into a café he would creep out again, because she stood before the bar – sometimes laughing, but more often silent, her head bent over her glass, her hair swinging; and about her people of every sort.

One night, coming home about three, he found her in the darkness, standing, back against the window, in the pod of the curtain, her chin so thrust forward that the muscles in her neck stood out. As he came toward her she said in a fury, 'I didn't want him!' Raising her hand she struck him across the face.

He stepped away, he dropped his monocle and caught at it swinging, he took his breath backward. He waited a whole second, trying to appear casual. 'You didn't want him,' he said. He bent down pretending to disentangle his ribbon, 'It seems I could not accomplish that.'

'Why not be secret about him?' she said. 'Why talk?'

Felix turned his body without moving his feet. 'What shall we do?'

She grinned, but it was not a smile. 'I'll get out,' she said. She took up her cloak, she always carried it dragging. She looked about her, about the room, as if she were seeing it for the first time.

For three or four months the people of the quarter asked for her in vain. Where she had gone no one knew. When she was seen again in the quarter, it was with Nora Flood. She did not explain where she had been, she was unable or unwilling to give an account of herself. The doctor said: 'In America, that's where Nora lives. I brought her into the world and I should know.'

CHAPTER THREE

Night Watch

The strangest 'salon' in America was Nora's. Her house was couched in the centre of a mass of tangled grass and weeds. Before it fell into Nora's hands the property had been in the same family two hundred years. It had its own burial ground, and a decaying chapel in which stood in tens and tens mouldering psalm books, laid down some fifty years gone in a flurry of forgiveness and absolution.

It was the 'paupers' salon, for poets, radicals, beggars, artists, and people in love; for Catholics, Protestants, Brahmins, dabblers in black magic and medicine; all these could be seen sitting about her oak table before the huge fire, Nora listening, her hand on her hound, the firelight throwing her shadow and his high against the wall. Of all that ranting roaring crew, she alone stood out. The equilibrium of her nature, savage and refined, gave her bridled skull a look of compassion. She was broad and tall, and though her skin was the skin of a child, there could be seen coming, early in her life, the design that was to be the weather-beaten grain of her face, that wood in the work; the tree coming forward in her, an undocumented record of time.

She was known instantly as a Westerner. Looking at her, foreigners remembered stories they had heard of covered wagons; animals going down to drink; children's heads, just as far as the eyes, looking in fright out of small windows, where in the dark another race crouched in ambush; with heavy hems the women becoming large, flattening the fields where they walked; God so ponderous in their minds that they could stamp out the world with him in seven days.

At these incredible meetings one felt that early American history was being re-enacted. The Drummer Boy, Fort Sumter, Lincoln, Booth, all somehow came to mind; Whigs and Tories were in the air; bunting and its stripes and stars, the swarm increasing slowly and accurately on the hive of blue; Boston tea tragedies, carbines, and the sound of a boy's wild calling; Puritan feet, long upright in the grave, striking the earth again, walking up and out of their custom; the calk of prayers thrust in the heart. And in the midst of this, Nora – sitting still, her hand on her dog, the firelight throwing her shadow against the wall, her head in shadow, bending as it reached the ceiling, though her own stood erect and motionless.

By temperament Nora was an early Christian; she believed the word. There is a gap in 'world pain' through which the singular falls continually and forever; a body falling in observable space, deprived of the privacy of disappearance; as if privacy, moving relentlessly away, by the very sustaining power of its withdrawal kept the body eternally moving downward, but in one place, and perpetually before the eye. Such a singular was Nora. There was some derangement in her equilibrium that kept her immune from her own descent.

Nora had the face of all people who love the people – a face that would be evil when she found out that to love without criticism is to be betrayed. Nora robbed herself for every one; incapable of giving herself warning, she was continually turning about to find herself diminished. Wandering people the world over found her profitable in that she could be sold for a price forever, for she carried her betrayal money in her own pocket.

Those who love everything are despised by everything, as those who love a city, in its profoundest sense, become the shame of that city, the *détraqués*, the paupers; their good is incommunicable, outwitted, being the rudiment of a life that has developed, as in man's body are found evidences of lost needs. This condition had struck even into Nora's house; it spoke in her guests, in her ruined gardens where she had been wax in every work of nature.

Wherever she was met, at the opera, at a play, sitting alone and apart, the programme face down on her knee, one would discover in her eyes, large, protruding and clear, that mirrorless look of polished metals which report not so much the object as the movement of the object. As the surface of a gun's barrel, reflecting a scene, will add to the image the portent of its construction, so her eyes contracted and fortified the play before her in her own unconscious terms. One sensed in the way she held her head that her ears were recording Wagner or Scarlatti, Chopin, Palestrina, or the lighter songs of the Viennese school, in a smaller but more intense orchestration.

And she was the only woman of the last century who could go up a hill with the Seventh Day Adventists and confound the seventh day – with a muscle in her heart so passionate that she made the seventh day immediate. Her fellow worshippers believed in that day and the end of the world out of a bewildered entanglement with the six days preceding it; Nora believed for the beauty of that day alone. She was by fate one of those people who are born unprovided for, except in the provision of herself.

One missed in her a sense of humour. Her smile was quick and definite, but disengaged. She chuckled now and again at a joke, but it was the amused grim chuckle of a person who looks up to discover that they have coincided with the needs of nature in a bird.

Cynicism, laughter, the second husk into which the shucked man crawls, she seemed to know little or nothing about. She was one of those deviations by which man thinks to reconstruct himself.

To 'confess' to her was an act even more secret than the communication provided by a priest. There was no ignominy in her; she recorded without reproach or accusation, being shorn of self-reproach or self-accusation. This drew people to her and frightened them; they could neither insult nor hold anything against her, though it embittered them to have to take back injustice that in her found no foothold. In court she would have been impossible; no one would have been hanged, reproached or forgiven, because no one would have been 'accused'. The world and its history were to Nora like a ship in a bottle; she herself was outside and unidentified, endlessly embroiled in a preoccupation without a problem.

Then she met Robin. The Denckman circus, which she kept in touch with even when she was not working with it (some of its people were visitors to her house), came into New York in the fall of 1923. Nora went alone. She came into the circle of the ring, taking her place in the front row.

Clowns in red, white and yellow, with the traditional smears on their faces, were rolling over the sawdust, as if they were in the belly of a great mother where there was yet room to play. A black horse, standing on trembling hind legs that shook in apprehension of the raised front hooves, his beautiful ribboned head pointed down and toward the trainer's whip, pranced slowly, the foreshanks flickering to the whip. Tiny dogs ran about trying to look like horses, then in came the elephants.

A girl sitting beside Nora took out a cigarette and lit it; her hands shook and Nora turned to look at her; she looked at her suddenly because the animals, going around and around the ring, all but climbed over at that point. They did not seem to see the girl, but as their dusty eyes moved past, the orbit of their light seemed to turn on her. At that moment Nora turned.

The great cage for the lions had been set up, and the lions were walking up and out of their small strong boxes into the arena. Ponderous and furred they came, their tails laid down across the floor, dragging and heavy, making the air seem full of withheld strength. Then as one powerful lioness came to the turn of the bars, exactly opposite the girl, she turned her furious great head with its yellow eyes afire and went down, her paws thrust through the bars and, as she regarded the girl, as if a river were falling behind impassable heat, her eyes flowed in tears that never reached the surface. At that the girl rose straight up. Nora took her hand. 'Let's get out of here!' the girl said, and still holding her hand Nora took her out.

In the lobby Nora said, 'My name is Nora Flood,' and she waited. After a pause the girl said, 'I'm Robin Vote.' She looked about her distractedly. 'I don't want to be here.' But it was all she said; she did not explain where she wished to be.

She stayed with Nora until the midwinter. Two spirits were working in her, love and anonymity. Yet they were so 'haunted' of each other that separation was impossible.

Nora closed her house. They travelled from Munich,

Vienna and Budapest into Paris. Robin told only a little of her life, but she kept repeating in one way or another her wish for a home, as if she were afraid she would be lost again, as if she were aware, without conscious knowledge, that she belonged to Nora, and that if Nora did not make it permanent by her own strength, she would forget.

Nora bought an apartment in the rue du Cherche-Midi. Robin had chosen it. Looking from the long windows one saw a fountain figure, a tall granite woman bending forward with lifted head, one hand was held over the pelvic round as if to warn a child who goes incautiously.

In the passage of their lives together every object in the garden, every item in the house, every word they spoke, attested to their mutual love, the combining of their humours. There were circus chairs, wooden horses bought from a ring of an old merry-go-round, venetian chandeliers from the Flea Fair, stage-drops from Munich, cherubim from Vienna, ecclesiastical hangings from Rome, a spinet from England, and a miscellaneous collection of music boxes from many countries; such was the museum of their encounter, as Felix's hearsay house had been testimony of the age when his father had lived with his mother.

When the time came that Nora was alone most of the night and part of the day, she suffered from the personality of the house, the punishment of those who collect their lives together. Unconsciously at first, she went about disturbing nothing; then she became aware that her soft and careful movements were the outcome of an unreasoning fear – if she disarranged anything Robin might become confused – might lose the scent of home.

Love becomes the deposit of the heart, analogous in all degrees to the 'findings' in a tomb. As in one will be charted the taken place of the body, the raiment, the utensils necessary to its other life, so in the heart of the lover will be traced, as an indelible shadow, that which he loves. In Nora's heart lay the fossil of Robin, intaglio of her identity, and about it for its maintenance ran Nora's blood. Thus the body of Robin could never be unloved, corrupt or put away. Robin was now beyond timely changes, except in the blood that animated her. That she could be spilled of this fixed the walking image of Robin in an appalling apprehension on Nora's mind – Robin alone, crossing streets, in danger. Her mind became so transfixed, that, by the agency of her fear, Robin seemed enormous and polarized, all catastrophes ran toward her, the magnetized predicament; and crying out, Nora would wake from sleep, going back through the tide of dreams into which her anxiety had thrown her, taking the body of Robin down with her into it, as the ground things take the corpse, with minute persistence, down into the earth, leaving a pattern of it on the grass, as if they stitched as they descended.

Yet now, when they were alone and happy, apart from the world in their appreciation of the world, there entered with Robin a company unaware. Sometimes it rang clear in the songs she sang, sometimes Italian, sometimes French or German, songs of the people, debased and haunting, songs that Nora had never heard before, or that she had never heard in company with Robin. When the cadence changed, when it was repeated on a lower key, she knew that Robin was singing of a life that she herself had no part in; snatches of harmony as tell-tale as the possessions of a traveller from a foreign land; songs like a practised whore who turns away from no one but the one who loves her. Sometimes Nora would sing them after Robin, with the trepidation of a foreigner repeating words in an unknown tongue, uncertain of what they may mean. Sometimes unable to endure the melody that told so much and so little, she would interrupt Robin with a question. Yet more distressing would be the moment, when, after a pause, the song would be taken up again, from an inner room where Robin, unseen, gave back an echo of her unknown life more nearly tuned to its origin. Often the song would stop altogether, until unthinking, just as she was leaving the house, Robin would break out again in anticipation, changing the sound from a reminiscence to an expectation.

Yet sometimes, going about the house, in passing each other, they would fall into an agonized embrace, looking into each other's face, their two heads in their four hands, so strained together that the space that divided them seemed to be thrusting them apart. Sometimes in these moments of insurmountable grief Robin would make some movement, use a peculiar turn of phrase not habitual to her, innocent of the betrayal, by which Nora was informed that Robin had come from a world to which she would return. To keep her (in Robin there was this tragic longing to be kept, knowing herself astray) Nora knew now that there was no way but death. In death Robin would belong to her. Death went with them, together and alone; and with the torment and catastrophe, thoughts of resurrection, the second duel.

Looking out into the fading sun of the winter sky, against which a little tower rose just outside the bedroom window, Nora would tabulate by the sounds of Robin dressing the exact progress of her toilet; chimes of cosmetic bottles and cream jars; the faint perfume of hair heated under the electric curlers; seeing in her mind the changing direction taken by the curls that hung on Robin's forehead, turning back from the low crown to fall in upward curves to the nape of the neck, the flat uncurved back head that spoke of some awful silence. Half narcoticized by the sounds and the knowledge that this was in preparation for departure, Nora spoke to herself: 'In the resurrection, when we come up looking backward at each other, I shall know you only of all that company. My ear shall turn in the socket of my head; my eyeballs loosened where I am the whirlwind about that cashed expense, my foot stubborn on the cast of your grave.' In the doorway Robin stood, 'Don't wait for me,' she said.

In the years that they lived together, the departures of Robin became a slowly increasing rhythm. At first Nora went with Robin; but as time passed, realizing that a growing tension was in Robin, unable to endure the knowledge that she was in the way or forgotten; seeing Robin go from table to table, from drink to drink, from person to person, realizing that if she herself were not there Robin might return to her as the one who, out of all the turbulent night, had not been lived through – Nora stayed at home, lying awake or sleeping. Robin's absence, as the night drew on, became a physical removal, insupportable and irreparable. As an amputated hand cannot be dis-owned, because it is experiencing a futurity, of which the victim is its forebear, so Robin was an amputation that Nora could not renounce. As the wrist longs, so her heart longed, and dressing she would go out into the night that she might be 'beside herself', skirting the café in which she would catch a glimpse of Robin.

Once out in the open Robin walked in a formless meditation, her hands thrust into the sleeves of her coat, directing her steps toward that night life that was a known measure between Nora and the cafés. Her meditations, during this walk, were a part of the pleasure she expected to find when the walk came to an end. It was this exact distance that kept the two ends of her life – Nora and the cafés – from forming a monster with two heads.

Her thoughts were in themselves a form of locomotion. She walked with raised head, seeming to look at every passer-by, yet her gaze was anchored in anticipation and regret. A look of anger, intense and hurried, shadowed her face and drew her mouth down as she neared her company; yet as her eyes moved over the façades of the buildings, searching for the sculptured head that both she and Nora loved (a Greek head with shocked protruding eyeballs, for which the tragic mouth seemed to pour forth tears), a quiet joy radiated from her own eyes; for this head was remembrance of Nora and her love, making the anticipation of the people she was to meet set and melancholy. So, without knowing she would do so, she took the turn that brought her into this particular street. If she was diverted, as was sometimes the case, by the interposition of a company of soldiers, a wedding or a funeral, then by her agitation she seemed a part of the function to the persons she stumbled against; as a moth by his very entanglement with the heat that shall be his extinction is associated with flame as a component part of its function. It was this characteristic that saved her from being asked too sharply 'where' she was going; pedestrians who had it on the point of their tongues, seeing her rapt and confused, turned instead to look at each other.

The doctor, seeing Nora out walking alone, said to himself, as the tall black-caped figure passed ahead of him under the lamps, 'There goes the dismantled – Love has fallen off her wall. A religious woman,' he thought to himself, 'without the joy and safety of the Catholic faith, which at a pinch covers up the spots on the wall when the family portraits take a slide; take that safety from a

54

woman,' he said to himself, quickening his step to follow her, 'and love gets loose and into the rafters. She sees her everywhere,' he added, glancing at Nora as she passed into the dark. 'Out looking for what she's afraid to find – Robin. There goes mother of mischief, running about, trying to get the world home.'

Looking at every couple as they passed, into every carriage and car, up to the lighted windows of the houses, trying to discover not Robin any longer, but traces of Robin, influences in her life (and those which were yet to be betrayed), Nora watched every moving figure for some gesture that might turn up in the movements made by Robin; avoiding the quarter where she knew her to be, where by her own movements the waiters, the people on the terraces might know that she had a part in Robin's life.

Returning home, the interminable night would begin. Listening to the faint sounds from the street, every murmur from the garden, an unevolved and tiny hum that spoke of the progressive growth of noise that would be Robin coming home, Nora lay and beat her pillow without force, unable to cry, her legs drawn up. At times she would get up and walk, to make something in her life outside more quickly over; to bring Robin back by the very velocity of the beating of her heart. And walking in vain, suddenly she would sit down on one of the circus chairs that stood by the long window overlooking the garden, bend forward, putting her hands between her legs, and begin to cry 'Oh, God! Oh, God! Oh, God!' repeated so often that it had the effect of all words spoken in vain. She nodded and awoke again and began to cry before she opened her eyes, and went back to the bed and fell into a dream which she recognized; though in the finality of this version she knew that the dream had not been 'well dreamt' before. Where

55

the dream had been incalculable, it was now completed with the entry of Robin.

Nora dreamed that she was standing at the top of a house, that is, the last floor but one – this was her Grandmother's room – an expansive, decaying splendour; yet somehow, though set with all the belongings of her grandmother, was as bereft as the nest of a bird which will not return. Portraits of her great-uncle, Llewellyn, who died in the Civil War, faded pale carpets, curtains that resembled columns from their time in stillness – a plume and an inkwell – the ink faded into the quill; standing, Nora looked down into the body of the house, as if from a scaffold, where now Robin had entered the dream, lying among a company below. Nora said to herself, 'The dream will not be dreamed again.' A disc of light, that seemed to come from some one or thing standing behind her and which was yet a shadow, shed a faintly luminous glow upon the upturned, still face of Robin who had the smile of an 'only survivor', a smile which fear had married to the bone.

From round about her in anguish Nora heard her own voice saying, 'Come up, this is Grandmother's room,' yet knowing it was impossible, because the room was taboo. The louder she cried out the farther away went the floor below, as if Robin and she, in their extremity, were a pair of opera glasses turned to the wrong end, diminishing in their painful love; a speed that ran away with the two ends of the building, stretching her apart.

This dream that now had all its parts, had still the former quality of never really having been her grandmother's room. She herself did not seem to be there in person, nor able to give an invitation. She had wanted to put her hands on something in this room to prove it; the dream had never permitted her to do so. This chamber that had never been her grandmother's, which was, on the contrary, the absolute opposite of any known room her grandmother had ever moved or lived in, was nevertheless saturated with the lost presence of her grandmother, who seemed in the continual process of leaving it. The architecture of dream had rebuilt her everlasting and continuous, flowing away in a long gown of soft folds and chin laces, the pinched gatherings that composed the train taking an upward line over the back and hips, in a curve that not only bent age but fear of bent age demands.

With this figure of her grandmother who was not entirely her recalled grandmother, went one of her childhood, when she had run into her at the corner of the house – the grandmother who, for some unknown reason, was dressed as a man, wearing a billycock and a corked moustache, ridiculous and plump in tight trousers and a red waistcoat, her arms spread saying with a leer of love, 'My little sweetheart!' – her grandmother 'drawn upon' as a prehistoric ruin is drawn upon, symbolizing her life out of her life, and which now appeared to Nora as something being done to Robin, Robin disfigured and eternalized by the hieroglyphics of sleep and pain.

Waking she began to walk again, and looking out into the garden in the faint light of dawn, she saw a double shadow falling from the statue, as if it were multiplying, and thinking perhaps this was Robin, she called and was not answered. Standing motionless, straining her eyes, she saw emerge from the darkness the light of Robin's eyes, the fear in them developing their luminosity until, by the intensity of their double regard, Robin's eyes and hers met. So they gazed at each other. As if that light had power to bring what was dreaded into the zone of their catastrophe, Nora saw the body of another woman swim up into the

57

statue's obscurity, with head hung down, that the added eyes might not augment the illumination; her arms about Robin's neck, her body pressed to Robin's, her legs slackened in the hang of the embrace.

Unable to turn her eyes away, incapable of speech, experiencing a sensation of evil, complete and dismembering, Nora fell to her knees, so that her eyes were not withdrawn by her volition, but dropped from their orbit by the falling of her body. Her chin on the sill she knelt thinking, 'Now they will not hold together,' feeling that if she turned away from what Robin was doing, the design would break and melt back into Robin alone. She closed her eyes, and at that moment she knew an awful happiness. Robin, like something dormant, was protected, moved out of death's way by the successive arms of women; but as she closed her eyes, Nora said 'Ah!' with the intolerable automatism of the last 'Ah!' in a body struck at the moment of its final breath.

CHAPTER FOUR

The Squatter

Jenny Petherbridge was a widow, a middle-aged woman who had been married four times. Each husband had wasted away and died; she had been like a squirrel racing a wheel day and night in an endeavour to make them historical; they could not survive it.

She had a beaked head and the body, small, feeble, and ferocious, that somehow made one associate her with Judy; they did not go together. Only severed could any part of her have been called 'right'. There was a trembling ardour in her wrists and fingers as if she were suffering from some elaborate denial. She looked old, yet expectant of age; she seemed to be steaming in the vapours of someone else about to die; still she gave off an odour to the mind (for there are purely mental smells that have no reality) of a woman about to be *accouchée*. Her body suffered from its fare, laughter and crumbs, abuse and indulgence. But put out a hand to touch her, and her head moved perceptibly with the broken arc of two instincts, recoil and advance, so that the head rocked timidly and aggressively at the same moment, giving her a slightly shuddering and expectant rhythm.

She writhed under the necessity of being unable to wear anything becoming, being one of those panicky little

59

women who, no matter what they put on, look like a child under penance.

She had a fancy for tiny ivory or jade elephants; she said they were luck; she left a trail of tiny elephants wherever she went; and she went hurriedly and gasping.

Her walls, her cupboards, her bureaux, were teeming with second-hand dealings with life. It takes a bold and authentic robber to get first-hand plunder. Someone else's marriage ring was on her finger; the photograph taken of Robin for Nora sat upon her table. The books in her library were other people's selections. She lived among her own things like a visitor to a room kept 'exactly as it was when—'. She tiptoed, even when she went to draw a bath, nervous and *andante*. She stopped, fluttering and febrile, before every object in her house. She had no sense of humour or peace or rest, and her own quivering uncertainty made even the objects which she pointed out to the company, as 'My virgin from Palma', or, 'the left-hand glove of La Duse', recede into a distance of uncertainty, so that it was almost impossible for the onlooker to see them at all. When anyone was witty about a contemporary event, she would look perplexed and a little dismayed, as if someone had done something that really should not have been done; therefore her attention had been narrowed down to listening for *faux pas*. She frequently talked about something being the 'death of her', and certainly anything could have been had she been the first to suffer it. The words that fell from her mouth seemed to have been lent to her; had she been forced to invent a vocabulary for herself, it would have been a vocabulary of two words, 'ah' and 'oh'. Hovering, trembling, tiptoeing, she would unwind anecdote after anecdote in a light rapid lisping voice which one always expected to change, to drop and to become the 'every day' voice; but it never did. The stories were humorous, well told. She would smile, toss her hands up, widen her eyes; immediately everyone in the room had a certain feeling of something lost, sensing that there was one person who was missing the importance of the moment, who had not heard the story; the teller herself.

She had endless cuttings and scraps from journals and old theatre programmes, haunted the Comédie Française, spoke of Molière, Racine and *La Dame aux Camélias*. She was generous with money. She made gifts lavishly and spontaneously. She was the worst recipient of presents in the world. She sent bushel baskets of camellias to actresses because she had a passion for the characters they portrayed. The flowers were tied with yards of satin ribbon, and a note accompanied them, effusive and gentle. To men she sent books by the dozen; the general feeling was that she was a well-read woman though she had read perhaps ten books in her life.

She had a continual rapacity for other people's facts; absorbing time, she held herself responsible for historic characters. She was avid and disorderly in her heart. She defiled the very meaning of personality in her passion to be a person; somewhere about her was the tension of the accident that made the beast the human endeavour.

She was nervous about the future, it made her indelicate. She was one of the most unimportantly wicked women of her time – because she could not let her time alone, and yet could never be a part of it. She wanted to be the reason for everything and so was the cause of nothing. She had the fluency of tongue and action meted out by divine providence to those who cannot think for themselves. She was master of the over-sweet phrase, the over-tight embrace.

One inevitably thought of her in the act of love emitting florid *commedia dell'arte* ejaculations; one should not have thought of her in the act of love at all. She thought of little else, and though always submitting to the act, spoke of and desired the spirit of love; yet was unable to attain it.

No one could intrude upon her, because there was no place for intrusion. This inadequacy made her insubordinate – she could not participate in a great love, she could only report it. Since her emotional reactions were without distinction, she had to fall back on the emotions of the past, great loves already lived and related, and over those she seemed to suffer and grow glad.

When she fell in love it was with a perfect fury of accumulated dishonesty; she became instantly a dealer in secondhand and therefore incalculable emotions. As, from the solid archives of usage, she had stolen or appropriated the dignity of speech, so she appropriated the most passionate love that she knew, Nora's for Robin. She was a 'squatter' by instinct.

Jenny knew about Nora immediately; to know Robin ten minutes was to know about Nora. Robin spoke of her in long, rambling, impassioned, sentences. It had caught Jenny by the ear – she listened, and both loves seemed to be one and her own. From that moment the catastrophe was inevitable. This was in 1927.

At their subsequent engagements, Jenny was always early and Robin late. Perhaps at the Ambassadeurs (Jenny feared meeting Nora). Perhaps dinner in the Bois – (Jenny had the collective income four dead husbands could afford) – Robin would walk in, with the aggressive slide to the foot common to tall people, slurred in its accent by the hipless smoothness of her gait – her hands in her pockets, the trench coat with the belt hanging, scowling and reluctant. Jenny leaning far over the table, Robin far back, her legs thrust under her, to balance the whole backward incline of the body, and Jenny so far forward that she had to catch her small legs in the back rung of the chair, ankle out and toe in, not to pitch forward on the table – thus they presented the two halves of a movement that had, as in sculpture, the beauty and the absurdity of a desire that is in flower but that can have no burgeoning, unable to execute its destiny; a movement that can divulge neither caution nor daring, for the fundamental condition for completion was in neither of them; they were like Greek runners, with lifted feet but without the relief of the final command that would bring the foot down – eternally angry, eternally separated, in a cataleptic frozen gesture of abandon.

The meeting at the opera had not been the first, but Jenny, seeing the doctor in the *promenoir*, aware of his passion for gossip, knew she had better make it seem so; as a matter of fact she had met Robin a year previously.

Though Jenny knew her safety lay in secrecy, she could not bear her safety; she wanted to be powerful enough to dare the world – and knowing she was not, the knowledge added to that already great burden of trembling timidity and fury.

On arriving at her house with the doctor and Robin, Jenny found several actresses awaiting her, two gentlemen, and the Marchesa de Spada, a very old rheumatic woman (with an antique spaniel, which suffered from asthma), who believed in the stars. There was talk about fate, and every hand in the room was searched and every destiny turned over and discussed. A little girl (Jenny called her niece, though she was no relation) sat at the far end of the room. She had been playing, but the moment Robin entered she ceased, and sat, her two small wax-like hands tender with the new life in them cupped up in her lap, staring under her long-lashed eyelids at no one else, as if she had become prematurely aware. This was the child Jenny spoke of later, when she called on Felix.

The Marchesa remarked that everyone in the room had been going on from interminable sources since the world began, and would continue to reappear, but that there was one person who had come to the end of her existence and would return no more. As she spoke, she looked slyly at Robin, who was standing by the piano speaking to the child in an undertone; and at the Marchesa's words Jenny began to tremble slightly, so that every point of her upstanding hair – it stood about her head in a bush, virile and unlovely – quivered. She began to pull herself along the enormous sofa towards the Marchesa, her legs under her, and suddenly she stood up.

'Order the carriages!' she cried. 'Immediately! We will go driving, we need a little air!' She turned her back and spoke in agitation. 'Yes, yes,' she said, 'the carriages! It is so close in here!'

'What carriages?' said the doctor, and he looked from one to the other. 'What carriages?' He could hear the maid unlocking the front door, calling out to the coachmen. He could hear the clear ringing sound of wheels drawn close to the kerb and the muttered cries of a foreign voice. Robin turned around and said, a malign gentle smile on her mouth, 'Now she is in a panic, and we will have to do something.' She put her glass down and stood, her back to the room, her broad shoulders drawn up, and though she was drunk, there was a withdrawal in her movement, and a wish to be gone.

'She will dress up now,' she said. She leaned back against the piano, pointing with the hand that held her glass. 'Dress up, wait, you will see.' Then she added, thrusting her chin forward so that the cords in her neck stood out: 'Dress up in something old.'

The doctor, who was more uncomfortable perhaps than anyone in the room and yet who could not forbear scandal, in order to gossip about the 'manifestations of our time' at a later date, made a slight gesture and said, 'Hush!' And sure enough, at that moment, Jenny appeared in the doorway to the bedroom, got up in a hoop, a bonnet and a shawl, and stood looking at Robin who was paying no attention to her, deep in conversation with the child. Jenny with the burning interest of a person who is led to believe herself a part of the harmony of a concert to which she is listening, appropriating in some measure its identity, emitted short, exclamatory ejaculations.

There were, it turned out, three carriages in all, those open hacks that may still be had in Paris if they are hunted up in time. Jenny had a standing order with them and when they were not called upon still they circled about her address, like flies about a bowl of cream. The three cabbies were hunched up on their boxes, their coats about their ears, for though it was an early autumn night, it had become very chilly by twelve o'clock. They had been ordered for eleven and had been sitting on their boxes for the past hour.

Jenny, cold with dread lest Robin should get into one of the other carriages with a tall slightly surprised English girl, seated herself in the farthest corner of the foremost *fiacre* and called, 'Here, here,' leaving the rest of the guests to dispose of themselves. The child, Sylvia, sat across from her, the ragged grey rug held in two clenched hands. There was a great deal of chattering and laughter, when to her horror Jenny saw that Robin was moving toward the second carriage in which the English girl had already seated herself. 'Ah no, no!' Jenny cried, and began beating the upholstery, sending up a cloud of dust. 'Come here,' she said in an anguished voice, as if it were the end of her life, 'Come here with me, both of you,' she added in a lowered and choking tone; and assisted by the doctor, Robin got in, the young Englishwoman, to Jenny's consternation, taking the seat by her side.

Dr O'Connor now turned to the driver and called out: '*Écoute, mon gosse, va comme si trente-six diables étaient accrochés à tes fesses!*' Then waving his hand in a gesture of abandon, he added: 'Where to but the woods, the sweet woods of Paris! *Fais le tour du Bois!*' he shouted, and slowly the three carriages, horse behind horse, moved out into the Champs-Elysées.

Jenny, with nothing to protect her against the night but her long Spanish shawl, which looked ridiculous over her flimsy hoop and bodice, a rug over her knees, had sunk back with collapsed shoulders. With darting, incredible swiftness, her eyes went from one girl to the other, while the doctor, wondering how he had managed to get himself into the carriage which held three women and a child, listened to the faint laughter from the carriages behind, feeling, as he listened, a twinge of occult misery. 'Ah!' he said under his breath. 'Just the girl that God forgot.' Saying which, he seemed to be precipitated into the halls of justice, where he had suffered twenty-four hours. 'Oh, God help us,' he said, speaking aloud, at which the child turned slightly on her seat, her head, with large intelligent eyes directed toward him, which had he noticed, would have silenced him instantly (for the doctor had a mother's reverence for childhood). 'What manner of man is it that has to adopt his brother's children to make a mother of himself, and sleeps with his brother's wife to get him a future – it's enough to bring down the black curse of Kerry.'

'What?' said Jenny in a loud voice, hoping to effect a break in the whispered conversation between Robin and the English girl. The doctor turned up his coat collar.

'I was saying, madame, that by his own peculiar perversity God has made me a liar–'

'What, what is that you say?' demanded Jenny, her eyes still fixed on Robin so that her question seemed to be directed rather to that corner of the carriage than to the doctor.

'You see before you, madame,' he said, 'one who was created in anxiety. My father, Lord rest his soul, had no happiness of me from the beginning. When I joined the army he relented a little because he had a suspicion that possibly in that fracas which occasionally puts a son on the list of "not much left since", I might be damaged. After all, he had no desire to see my ways corrected with a round of buckshot. He came into me early in the dawn as I lay in my bed, to say that he forgave me, and that indeed he hoped to be forgiven; that he had never understood, but that he had, by much thought, by heavy reading, come back with love in his hand, that he was sorry, that he came to say so; that he hoped I could conduct myself like a soldier. For a moment he seemed to realize my terrible predicament: to be shot for man's meat, but to go down like a girl, crying in the night for her mother. So I got up in bed on my knees and crawled to the foot where he stood, and cast my arms about him and said, "No matter what you have done or thought, you were right, and there's nothing in my heart but love for you and respect."'

Jenny had shrunk into her rug and was not listening. Her eyes followed every movement of Robin's hand, which was laid now on the child's hand, now stroking her hair, the child smiling up into the trees.

'Oh,' said the doctor, 'for the love of God!'

Jenny began to cry slowly, the tears wet, warm and sudden in the odd misery of her face. It made the doctor sad, with that unhappy yet pleasantly regrettable discomfort on which he usually launched his better meditations.

He remarked, and why he did not know, that by weeping she appeared like a single personality, who, by multiplying her tears, brought herself into the position of one who is seen twenty times in twenty mirrors – still only one, but many times distressed. Jenny began to weep outright. As the initial soft weeping had not caught Robin's attention, now Jenny used the increase and the catching in her throat to attract her, with the same insistent fury one feels when trying to attract a person in a crowded room. The weeping became as accurate as the monotonous underplay in a score, in spite of the incapacity of her heart. The doctor, sitting now a little slumped forward, said, in an almost professional voice (they were now long past the pond and the park, and were circling back again, toward the lower parts of town), 'Love of woman for woman, what insane passion for unmitigated anguish and motherhood brought that into the mind?'

'Oh, oh,' she said, 'Look at her!' She abruptly made a gesture toward Robin and the girl, as if they were no longer present, as if they were a vista passing out of view with the movement of the horses. 'Look, she brings love down to a level!' She hoped that Robin would hear.

'Ah!' he said. 'Love, that terrible thing!'

She began to beat the cushions with her doubled fist. 'What could you know about it? Men never know anything about it, why should they? But a woman should know – they are finer, more sacred; my love is sacred and my love is great!'

'Shut up,' Robin said, putting her hand on her knee. 'Shut up, you don't know what you are talking about. You talk all the time and you never know anything. It's such an

68

awful weakness with you. Identifying yourself with God!' She was smiling, and the English girl, breathing very quickly, lit a cigarette. The child remained speechless, as she had been for the duration of the drive, her head turned as if fixed, looking at Robin, and trying to hold her slight legs, that did not reach the floor, from shaking with the shaking of the carriage.

Then Jenny struck Robin, scratching and tearing in hysteria, striking, clutching and crying. Slowly the blood began to run down Robin's cheeks, and as Jenny struck repeatedly Robin began to go forward as if brought to the movement by the very blows themselves, as if she had no will, sinking down in the small carriage, her knees on the floor, her head forward as her arm moved upward in a gesture of defence; and as she sank, Jenny also, as if compelled to conclude the movement of the first blow, almost as something seen in retarded action, leaned forward and over, so that when the whole of the gesture was completed, Robin's hands were covered by Jenny's slight and bending breast, caught in between the bosom and the knees. And suddenly the child flung herself down on the seat, face outward, and said in a voice not suitable for a child, because it was controlled with terror: 'Let me go! Let me go! Let me go!'

The carriage at this moment drew smartly up into the rue du Cherche-Midi. Robin jumped before the carriage stopped, but Jenny was close behind her, following her as far as the garden.

It was not long after this that Nora and Robin separated; a little later Jenny and Robin sailed for America.

CHAPTER FIVE

Watchman, What of the Night?

About three in the morning, Nora knocked at the little glass door of the concierge's *loge*, asking if the doctor was in. In the anger of broken sleep the concierge directed her to climb six flights, where at the top of the house, to the left, she would find him.

Nora took the stairs slowly. She had not known that the doctor was so poor. Groping her way she rapped, fumbling for the knob. Misery alone would have brought her, though she knew the late hours indulged in by her friend. Hearing his 'come in' she opened the door and for one second hesitated, so incredible was the disorder that met her eyes. The room was so small that it was just possible to walk sideways up to the bed, it was as if being condemned to the grave the doctor had decided to occupy it with the utmost abandon.

A pile of medical books, and volumes of a miscellaneous order, reached almost to the ceiling, water-stained and covered with dust. Just above them was a very small barred window, the only ventilation. On a maple dresser, certainly not of European make, lay a rusty pair of forceps, a broken scalpel, half a dozen odd instruments that she could not place, a catheter, some twenty perfume bottles, almost empty, pomades, creams, rouges, powder boxes and puffs.

From the half-open drawers of this chiffonnier hung laces, ribands, stockings, ladies' underclothing and an abdominal brace, which gave the impression that the feminine finery had suffered venery. A swill-pail stood at the head of the bed, brimming with abominations. There was something appallingly degraded about the room, like the rooms in brothels, which give even the most innocent a sensation of having been accomplice; yet this room was also muscular, a cross between a *chambre à coucher* and a boxer's training camp. There is a certain belligerence in a room in which a woman has never set foot; every object seems to be battling its own compression – and there is a metallic odour, as of beaten irony in a smithy.

In the narrow iron bed, with its heavy and dirty linen sheets, lay the doctor in a woman's flannel nightgown.

The doctor's head, with its over-large black eyes, its full gunmetal cheeks and chin, was framed in the golden semi-circle of a wig with long pendent curls that touched his shoulders, and falling back against the pillow, turned up the shadowy interior of their cylinders. He was heavily rouged and his lashes painted. It flashed into Nora's head: 'God, children know something they can't tell, they like Red Riding Hood and the wolf in bed!' But this thought, which was only the sensation of a thought, was of but a second's duration, as she opened the door; in the next, the doctor had snatched the wig from his head, and sinking down in the bed drew the sheets up over his breast. Nora said, as quickly as she could recover herself: 'Doctor, I have come to ask you to tell me everything you know about the night.' As she spoke, she wondered why she was so dismayed to have come upon the doctor at the hour when he had evacuated custom and gone back into his dress. The doctor said, 'You see that you can ask me anything,' thus laying aside both their embarrassments. She said to herself: 'Is not the gown the natural raiment of extremity? What nation, what religion, what ghost, what dream has not worn it – infants, angels, priests, the dead; why should not the doctor, in the grave dilemma of his alchemy, wear his dress?' She thought: 'He dresses to lie beside himself, who is so constructed that love, for him, can be only something special; in a room that giving back evidence of his occupancy, is as mauled as the last agony.'

'Have you ever thought of the night?' the doctor inquired with a little irony; he was extremely put out, having expected someone else, though his favourite topic, and one which he talked on whenever he had a chance, was the night. 'Yes,' said Nora, and sat down on the only chair. 'I've thought of it, but thinking about something you know nothing about does not help.'

'Have you,' said the doctor, 'ever thought of the peculiar polarity of times and times; and of sleep? Sleep the slain white bull? Well, I, doctor Matthew-Mighty-grain-of-salt-Dante-O'Connor, will tell you how the day and the night are related by their division. The very constitution of twilight is a fabulous reconstruction of fear, fear bottom-out and wrong side up. Every day is thought upon and calculated, but the night is not premeditated. The Bible lies the one way, but the nightgown the other. The Night, "Beware of that dark door!"'

'I used to think,' Nora said, 'that people just went to sleep, or if they did not go to sleep, that they were themselves, but now,' she lit a cigarette and her hands trembled, 'now I see that the night does something to a person's identity, even when asleep.'

'Ah!' exclaimed the doctor. 'Let a man lay himself down in the Great Bed and his "identity" is no longer his own, his "trust" is not with him, and his "willingness" is turned over and is of another permission. His distress is wild and anonymous. He sleeps in a Town of Darkness, member of a secret brotherhood. He neither knows himself nor his outriders, he berserks a fearful dimension and dismounts, miraculously, in bed!

'His heart is tumbling in his chest, a dark place! Though some go into the night as a spoon breaks easy water, others go head foremost against a new connivance; their horns make a dry crying, like the wings of the locust, late come to their shedding.

'Have you thought of the night, now, in other times, in foreign countries – in Paris? When the streets were gall high with things you wouldn't have done for a dare's sake, and the way it was then; with the pheasants' necks and the goslings' beaks dangling against the hocks of the gallants, and not a pavement in the place, and everything gutters for miles and miles, and a stench to it that plucked you by the nostrils and you were twenty leagues out! The criers telling the price of wine to such good effect that the dawn saw good clerks full of piss and vinegar, and blood-letting in side streets where some wild princess in a night shift of velvet howled under a leech; not to mention the palaces of Nymphenburg echoing back to Vienna with the night trip of late kings letting water into plush cans and fine wood-work, no,' he said looking at her sharply, 'I can see you have not! You should, for the night has been going on for a long time.'

She said, 'I've never known it before – I thought I did, but it was not knowing at all.'

'Exactly,' said the doctor, 'you thought you knew, and you hadn't even shuffled the cards – now the nights of one period are not the nights of another. Neither are the nights of one city the nights of another. Let us take Paris for an instance, and France for a fact. *Ah, Mon Dieu! La nuit effroyable! La nuit, qui est une immense plaine, el le coeur qui est une petite extrémité!* Ah, good Mother mine, *Notre Dame-de-bonne-Garde!* Intercede for me now, while yet I explain what I'm coming to! French nights are those which all nations seek the world over – and have you noticed that? Ask doctor Mighty O'Connor; the reason the doctor knows everything is because he's been everywhere at the wrong time and has now become anonymous.'

'But,' Nora said, 'I never thought of the night as a life at all – I've never lived it – why did she?'

'I'm telling you of French nights at the moment,' the doctor went on, 'and why we all go into them. The night and the day are two travels, and the French – gut-greedy and fist-tight though they often are – alone leave testimony of the two in the dawn; we tear up the one for the sake of the other, not so the French.

'And why is that, because they think of the two as one continually, and keep it before their mind as the monks who repeat, "Lord Jesus Christ, Son of God, have mercy upon me!" Some twelve thousand or more times a twenty-four hours, so that it is finally in the head, good or bad, without saying a word. Bowing down from the waist, the world over they go, that they may revolve about the Great Enigma – as a relative about a cradle – and the Great Enigma can't be thought of unless you turn the head the other way, and come upon thinking with the eye that you fear, which is called the back of the head; it's the one we use when looking at the beloved in a dark place, and she is a long time coming from a great way. We swoon with the thickness of our own tongue when we say, "I love you," as in the eye of a child lost a long while will be found the contraction of that distance – a child going small in the claws of a beast, coming furiously up the furlongs of the iris. We are but skin about a wind, with muscles clenched against mortality. We sleep in a long reproachful dust against ourselves. We are full to the gorge with our own names for misery. Life, the pastures in which the night feeds and prunes the cud that nourishes us to despair. Life, the permission to know death. We were created that the earth might be made sensible of her inhuman taste; and love that the body might be so dear that even the earth should roar with it. Yes, we who are full to the gorge with misery, should look well around, doubting everything seen, done, spoken, precisely because we have a word for it, and not its alchemy.

'To think of the acorn it is necessary to become the tree. And the tree of night is the hardest tree to mount, the dourest tree to scale, the most difficult of branch, the most febrile to the touch, and sweats a resin and drips a pitch against the palm that computation has not gambled. Gurus, who, I trust you know, are Indian teachers, expect you to contemplate the acorn ten years at a stretch, and if, in that time, you are no wiser about the nut, you are not very bright, and that may be the only certainty with which you will come away, which is a post-graduate melancholy – for no man can find a greater truth than his kidney will allow. So I, doctor Matthew Mighty O'Connor, ask you to think of the night the day long, and of the day the night through, or at some reprieve of the brain it will come upon you heavily – an engine stalling itself upon your chest, halting its wheels against your heart; unless you have made a roadway for it.

'The French have made a detour of filthiness – Oh, the good dirt! Whereas you are of a clean race, of a too eagerly washing people, and this leaves no road for you. The brawl of the Beast leaves a path for the Beast. You wash your brawl with every thought, with every gesture, with every conceivable emollient and savon, and expect to find your way again. A Frenchman makes a navigable hour with a tuft of hair, a wrenched *bretelle*, a rumpled bed. The tear of wine is still in his cup to catch back the quantity of its bereavement, his *cantiques* straddle two backs, night and day.'

'But, what am I to do?' she said.

'Be as the Frenchman, who puts a sou in the poor box at night that he may have a penny to spend in the morning – he can trace himself back by his sediment, vegetable and animal, and so find himself in the odour of wine in its two travels, in and out, packed down beneath an air that has not changed its position during that strategy.

'The American, what then? He separates the two for fear of indignities, so that the mystery is cut in every cord; the design wildcats down the *charter mortalis*, and you get crime. The startled bell in the stomach begins to toll, the hair moves and drags upward, and you go far away backward by the crown, your conscience belly out and shaking.

'Our bones ache only while the flesh is on them. Stretch it as thin as the temple flesh of an ailing woman and still it serves to ache the bone and to move the bone about; and in like manner the night is a skin pulled over the head of day that the day may be in a torment. We will find no comfort until the night melts away; until the fury of the night rots out its fire.'

'Then,' Nora said, 'It means – I'll never understand her – I'll always be miserable – just like this.'

'Listen! Do things look in the ten and twelve of noon as they look in the dark? Is the hand, the face, the foot, the same face and hand and foot seen by the sun? For now the hand lies in a shadow, its beauties and its deformities are in a smoke – there is a sickle of doubt across the cheekbone thrown by the hat's brim, so there is half a face to be peered back into speculation. A leaf of darkness has fallen under the chin and lies deep upon the arches of the eyes; the eyes themselves have changed their colour. The very mother's head you swore by in the dock is a heavier head, crowned with ponderable hair.

'And what of the sleep of animals? The great sleep of the elephant, and the fine thin sleep of the bird?'

Nora said: 'I can't stand it, I don't know how – I am frightened. What is it? What is it in her that is doing this?'

'Oh, for God's sake!' the doctor said, 'give me the smelling salts.' She got up, looking among the debris on the stand. Inhaling, he pushed his head back into the pillow, then he said:

'Take history at night, have you ever thought of that, now? Was it at night that Sodom became Gomorrah? It was at night, I swear! A city given over to the shades, and that's why it has never been countenanced or understood to this day. Wait, I'll be coming to that! All through the night Rome went burning. Put that in the noontide and it loses some of its age-old significance, does it not? Why? Because it has existed to the eye of the mind all these years against a black sky. Burn Rome in a dream, and you reach and claw down the true calamity. For dreams have only the pigmentation of fact. A man who has to deal in no colour cannot find his match, or, if he does, it is for a different rage. Rome was the egg, but colour was the tread.'

'Yes,' said Nora.

'The dead have committed some portion of the evil of the night; sleep and love, the other. For what is not the sleeper

77

responsible? What converse does he hold, and with whom? He lies down with his Nelly and drops off into the arms of his Gretchen. Thousands unbidden come to his bed. Yet how can one tell truth when it's never in the company? Girls that the dreamer has not fashioned himself to want, scatter their legs about him to the blows of Morpheus. So used is he to sleep that the dream that eats away its boundaries finds even what is dreamed an easier custom with the years, and at that banquet the voices blend and battle without pitch. The sleeper is the proprietor of an unknown land. He goes about another business in the dark – and we, his partners, who go to the opera, who listen to gossip of café friends, who walk along the boulevards, or sew a quiet seam, cannot afford an inch of it; because, though we would purchase it with blood, it has no counter and no till. She who stands looking down upon her who lies sleeping knows the horizontal fear, the fear unbearable. For man goes only perpendicularly against his fate. He was neither formed to know that other nor compiled of its conspiracy.

'You beat the liver out of a goose to get a *pâté*; you pound the muscles of a man's *cardia* to get a philosopher.'

'Is that what I am to learn?' she asked bitterly.

The doctor looked at her. 'For the lover, it is the night into which his beloved goes,' he said, 'that destroys his heart; he wakes her suddenly, only to look the hyena in the face that is her smile, as she leaves that company.

'When she sleeps is she not moving her leg aside for an unknown garrison? Or in a moment, that takes but a second, murdering us with an axe? Eating our ear in a pie, pushing us aside with the back of her hand, sailing to some port with a ship full of sailors and medical men? And what of our own sleep? We go to it no better – and betray her with the very virtue of our days. We are continent a long time, but no sooner has our head touched the pillow, and our eyes left the day, than a host of merrymakers take and get. We wake from our doings in a deep sweat for that they happened in a house without an address, in a street in no town, citizened with people with no names with which to deny them. Their very lack of identity makes them ourselves. For by a street number, by a house, by a name, we cease to accuse ourselves. Sleep demands of us a guilty immunity. There is not one of us who, given an eternal incognito, a thumbprint nowhere set against our souls, would not commit rape, murder and all abominations. For if pigeons flew out of his bum, or castles sprang out of his ears, man would be troubled to know which was his fate, a house, a bird or a man. Possibly that one only who shall sleep three generations will come up uninjured out of that unpeopled annihilation.' The doctor turned heavily in bed.

'For the thickness of the sleep that is on the sleeper we "forgive", as we "forgive" the dead for the account of the earth that lies upon them. What we do not see, we are told, we do not mourn; yet night and sleep trouble us, suspicion being the strongest dream and dread the thong. The heart of the jealous knows the best and the most satisfying love, that of the other's bed, where the rival perfects the lover's imperfections. Fancy gallops to take part in that duel, unconstrained by any certain articulation of the laws of that unseen game.

'We look to the East for a wisdom that we shall not use – and to the sleeper for the secret that we shall not find. So, I say, what of the night, the terrible night? The darkness is the closet in which your lover roosts her heart, and that night fowl that caws against her spirit and yours, dropping between you and her the awful estrangement of his bowels. The drip of your tears in his implacable pulse. Night people do not bury their dead, but on the neck of you, their beloved and waking, sling the creature, husked of its gestures. And where you go, it goes, the two of you, your living and her dead, that will not die; to daylight, to life, to grief, until both are carrion.

'Wait! I'm coming to the night of nights – the night you want to know about the most of all – for even the greatest generality has a little particular; have you thought of that? A high price is demanded of any value, for a value is in itself a detachment! We wash away our sense of sin, and what does that bath secure us? Sin, shining bright and hard. In what does a Latin bathe? True dust. We have made the literal error. We have used water, we are thus too sharply reminded. A European gets out of bed with a disorder that holds the balance. The layers of his deed can be traced back to the last leaf and the good slug be found creeping. *L'Echo de Paris* and his bed sheets were run off the same press. One may read in both the travail life has had with him – he reeks with the essential wit necessary to the "sale" of both editions, night edition and day.

'Each race to its wrestling! Some throw the beast on the other side, with the stench of excrement, blood and flowers, the three essential oils of their plight! Man makes his history with the one hand and "holds it up" with the other.

'Oh, God, I'm tired of this tirade. The French are dishevelled, and wise, the American tries to approximate it with drink. It is his only clue to himself. He takes it when his soap has washed him too clean for identification. The Anglo-Saxon has made the literal error; using water, he has washed away his page. Misery melts him down by day, and sleep at night. His preoccupation with his business day has made his sleep insoluble.'

Nora stood up, but she sat down again. 'How do you

stand it, then?' she demanded. 'How do you live at all, if this wisdom of yours is not only the truth, but also the price?'

'Ho, nocturnal hag whimpering on the thorn, rot in the grist, mildew in the corn,' said the doctor. 'If you'll pardon my song and singing voice, both of which were better until I gave my kidney on the left side to France in the war – and I've drunk myself half around the world cursing her for jerking it out – if I had it to do again, grand country though it is – I'd be the girl found lurking behind the army, or up with the hill folk, all of which is to rest me a little of my knowledge, until I can get back to it. I'm coming to something. *Misericordia*, am I not the girl to know of what I speak? We go to our Houses by our nature – and our nature, no matter how it is, we all have to stand – as for me, so God has made me, my house is the pissing port. Am I to blame if I've been summoned before and this my last and oddest call? In the old days I was possibly a girl in Marseilles thumping the dock with a sailor, and perhaps it's the memory that haunts me. The wise men say that the remembrance of things past is all that we have for a future, and am I to blame if I've turned up this time as I shouldn't have been, when it was a high soprano I wanted, and deep corn curls to my bum, with a womb as big as the king's kettle, and a bosom as high as the bowsprit of a fishing schooner? And what do I get but a face on me like an old child's bottom – is that a happiness, do you think?

'Jehovah, Sabaoth, Elohim, Eloi, Helion, Jodhevah, Shaddai! May God give us to die in our own way! I haunt the *pissoirs* as naturally as Highland Mary her cows down by the Dee – and by the Hobs of Hell, I've seen the same thing work in a girl. But I'll bring that up later! I've given my destiny away by garrulity, like ninety per cent of everybody else – for, no matter what I may be doing, in my heart is the wish for children and knitting. God, I never asked better than to boil some good man's potatoes and toss up a child for him every nine months by the calendar. Is it my fault that my only fireside is the outhouse? And that I can never hang my muffler, mittens and Bannybrook umbrella on anything better than a bit of tin boarding as high as my eyes, having to be brave, no matter what, to keep the mascara from running away? And do you think that those circular cottages have not brought me to great argument? Have you ever glanced at one when the night was well down, and seen it and what it looked like and resembled most, with its one coping and a hundred legs? A centipede. And you look down and choose your feet, and, ten to one, you find a bird with a light wing, or an old duck with a wooden knee, or something that has been mournful for years. What? I've held argument with others at long tables all night through about the particular merits of one district over another for such things, of one cottage over another for such things. And do you suppose I was agreed with, and had any one any other one's ideas? There was as much disagreement as there might have been, had we all been selecting a new order of government. Jed would say North, and Jod would say South, and me sitting between them going mad because I am a doctor and a collector and a talker of Latin, and a sort of petropus of the twilight and a physiognomist that can't be flustered by the wrong feature on the right face, and I said that the best port was at the Place de la Bastille. Whereupon I was torn into parts by a hundred voices – each of them pitched in a different *arrondissement*, until I began clapping like the good woman in the shoe, and screaming for silence; and for witchery I banged the table with a *formidable*, and yelled out loud: "Do any of you know anything about atmosphere and sea level? Well," I says, "sea level, and atmospheric pressure and topography make all the difference in the world!" My voice cracked on the word "difference", soaring up divinely, and I said: "If you think that certain things do not show from what district they come, yea, even to an *arrondissement*, then you are not out gunning for particular game, but simply any catch, and I'll have nothing to do with you! I do not discuss weighty matters with water wits!" And at that I ordered another and sat with my chin up. "But," said one fellow, "it's the face that you tell by." "Faces is it!" I screamed, "the face is for fools! If you fish by the face you fish out trouble, but there's always other fish when you deal with the sea. The face is what anglers catch in the daylight, but the sea is the night!"'

Nora turned away – 'What am I to do?'

'Ah, mighty uncertainty!' said the doctor. 'Have you thought of all the doors that have shut at night and opened again? Of women who have looked about with lamps, like you, and who have scurried on fast feet? Like a thousand mice they go this way and that, now fast, now slow, some halting behind doors, some trying to find the stairs, all approaching or leaving their misplaced mouse meat, that lies in some cranny, on some couch, down on some floor, behind some cupboard; and all the windows, great and small, from which love and fear have peered, shining and in tears? Put those windows end to end and it would be a casement that would reach around the world; and put those thousand eyes into one eye and you would have the night combed with the great blind searchlight of the heart.'

Tears began to run down Nora's face.

'And do I know my Sodomites?' the doctor said unhappily, 'and what the heart goes bang up against if it loves one of them, especially if it's a woman loving one of them. What do they find then, that this lover has committed the unpardonable error of not being able to exist – and they come down with a dummy in their arms. God's last round, shadow-boxing, that the heart may be murdered and swept into that still quiet place where it can sit and say: "Once I was, now I can rest."

'Well, that's only part of it,' he said, trying to stop her crying, 'and though your normal fellow will say all are alike in the dark, negro or white, I say you can tell them, and where they came from, and what quarter they frequent, by the size and excellence – and at the Bastille (and may I be believed) they come as handsome as mortadellas slung on a table.

'Your *gourmet* knows for instance from what water his fish was snatched, he knows from what district and to what year he blesses his wine, he knows one truffle from another and whether it be Brittany root or if it came down from the North, but you gentlemen sit here and tell me that the district makes no difference – is there no one who knows anything but myself? And, must I, perchance, like careful writers, guard myself against the conclusions of my readers?

'Have I not shut my eyes with the added shutter of the night and put my hand out? And it's the same with girls,' he said, 'those who turn the day into night, the young, the drug addict, the profligate, the drunken and that most miserable, the lover who watches all night long in fear and anguish. These can never again live the life of the day. When one meets them at high noon they give off, as if it were a protective emanation, something dark and muted. The light does not become them any longer. They begin to have an unrecorded look. It is as if they were being tried by the continual blows of an unseen adversary. They acquire an "unwilling" set of features: they become old without reward, the widower bird sitting sighing at the turnstile of heaven. "Hallelujah! I am sticked! *Skoll! Skoll!* I am dying!"

'Or walks the floor, holding her hands; or lies upon the floor, face down, with that terrible longing of the body that would, in misery, be flat with the floor; lost lower than burial, utterly blotted out and erased so that no stain of her could ache upon the wood, or snatched back to nothing without aim – going backward through the target, taking with her the spot where she made one—'

'Yes!' Nora said.

'Look for the girls also in the toilets at night, and you will find them kneeling in that great secret confessional crying between tongues, the terrible excommunication:

'"May you be damned to hell! May you die standing upright! May you be damned upward! May this be damned, terrible and damned spot! May it wither into the grin of the dead, may this draw back, low riding mouth in an empty snarl of the groin! May this be your torment, may this be your damnation! God damned me before you, and after me you shall be damned, kneeling and standing away till we vanish! For what do you know of me, man's meat? I'm an angel on all fours, with a child's feet behind me, seeking my people that have never been made, going down face foremost, drinking the waters of night at the water hole of the damned, and I go into the waters, up to my heart, the terrible waters! What do you know of me? May you pass from me, damned girl! Damned and betraying!"

'There's a curse for you,' he said, 'and I have heard it.'

'Oh!' Nora said, 'Don't – don't!'

'But,' he continued, 'if you think that is all of the night, you're crazy! Groom, bring the shovel! Am I the golden-mouthed St John Chrysostom, the Greek who said it with the other cheek? No, I'm a fart in a gale of wind, a humble violet, under a cow pad. But,' he said with sorrow, 'even that evil in us comes to an end, errors may make you immortal – one woman went down the ages for sitting through *Parsifal* up to the point where the swan got his death, whereupon she screamed out "Godamercy, they have shot the Holy Grail!" —but not every one is as good as that; you lay up for yourself in your old age, Nora, my child, feebleness enough to forget the passions of your youth, which you spent your years in strengthening. Think of that also. As for me, I tuck myself in at night, well content because I am my own charlatan. Yes, I, the Lily of Killarney, am composing me a new song, with tears and with jealousy, because I have read that John was his favourite, and it should have been me, Prester Matthew! The song is entitled, "Mother, put the wheel away, I cannot spin tonight." Its other name, "According to me, everyone is a kind-of-a-son-of-a-bitch," to be sung to two ocarinas and one concertina, and, if none of the world is about, to a Jew's-harp, so help me God! I am but a little child with my eyes wide open!'

'Matthew,' Nora said, 'what will become of her? That's what I want to know.'

'To our friends,' he answered, 'we die every day, but to ourselves we die only at the end. We do not know death, or how often it has essayed our most vital spirit. While we are in the parlour it is visiting in the pantry. Montaigne says: "To kill a man there is required a bright shining and clear light," but that was spoken of the conscience toward another man. But what of our own death – permit us to reproach the night, wherein we die manifold alone. Donne says: "We are all conceived in close prison, in our mothers' wombs we are close prisoners all. When we are born, we are but born to the liberty of the house – all our life is but a going out to the place of execution and death. Now was there ever any man seen to sleep in the Cart, between Newgate and Tyburn? Between the prison and the place of execution, does any man sleep?" Yet he says, "men sleep all the way". How much more, therefore, is there upon him a close sleep when he is mounted on darkness." '

'Yes,' she said, 'but –'

'Now, wait a minute! It's all of a certain night that I'm coming to, that I take so long coming to it,' he said, 'a night in the branchy pitch of fall – the particular night you want to know about – for I'm a fisher of men and my gimp is doing a *saltarello* over every body of water to fetch up what it may. I have a narrative, but you will be put to it to find it.

'Sorrow fiddles the ribs and no man should put his hand on anything; there is no direct way. The foetus of symmetry nourishes itself on cross purposes, this is its wonderful unhappiness – and now I am come to Jenny – oh, Lord, why do women have partridge blood and set out to beat up trouble? The places Jenny moults in are her only distinction, a Christian with a wanderer's rump. She smiles, and it is the wide smile of the self-abused, radiating to the face from some localized centre disturbance, the personification of the "thief". She has a longing for other people's property, but the moment she possesses it the property loses some of its value, for the owner's estimate is its worth. Therefore it was she took your Robin.'

'What is she like?' Nora asked.

'Well,' said the doctor, 'I have always thought I, myself, the funniest looking creature on the face of the earth; then I laid my eyes on Jenny – a little, hurried decaying comedy jester, the face on the fool's stick, and with a smell about her of mouse-nests. She is a "looter", and eternally nervous.

Even in her sleep I'll pronounce that her feet twitch and her orifices expand and contract like the iris of a suspicious eye. She speaks of people taking away her "faith" in them, as if faith were a transportable object – all her life she has been subject to the feeling of "removal". Were she a soldier she would define defeat with the sentence: "The enemy took the war away." Having a conviction that she is somehow reduced, she sets about collecting a destiny – and for her, the sole destiny is love, anyone's love and so her own. So only someone's love is her love. The cock crew and she was laid – her present is always someone else's past, jerked out and dangling.

'Yet what she steals she keeps, through the incomparable fascination of maturation and rot. She has the strength of an incomplete accident – one is always waiting for the rest of it, for the last impurity that will make the whole; she was born at the point of death, but, unfortunately, she will not age into youth – which is a grave mistake of nature. How more tidy had it been to have been born old and have aged into a child, brought finally to the brink, not of the grave, but of the womb; in our age bred up into infants searching for a womb to crawl into, not be made to walk loth the gingerly dust of death, but to find a moist, gill-flirted way. And a funny sight it would be to see us going to our separate lairs at the end of day, women wincing with terror, not daring to set foot to the street for fear of it.

'But I'm coming by degrees to the narrative of the one particular night that makes all other nights seem like something quite decent enough – and that the night when, dressed in open-work mittens, showing the edge of a pantaloon (and certainly they had been out of style three mothers behind her), Jenny Petherbridge – for that is her name in case you'd care to know it,' he said with a grin, 'wrapped in a shawl of Spanish insight and Madrid fancy (as a matter of fact, the costume came later, but what do I care?), stepped out in the early fall of the year to the Opera – I think, and I am not mistaken, it was nothing better than *Rigoletto* – walking in the galleries and whisking her eyes about for trouble – that she swore, even after, she had really never wanted to know anything about – and there laid her eyes on Robin, who was leaning forward in a box, and me pacing up and down, talking to myself in the best Comédie Française French, trying to keep off what I knew was going to be trouble for a generation, and wishing I was hearing the Schumann cycle – when in swishes the old sow of a Danish count. My heart aches for all poor creatures putting on dog and not a pot to piss in or a window to throw it from. And I began to think, and I don't know why, of the closed gardens of the world where all people can make their thoughts go up high because of the narrowness and beauty, or of the wide fields where the heart can spread out and thin its vulgarity (it's why I eat salad), and I thought, we should all have a place to throw our flowers in, like me who, once in my youth, rated a *corbeille* of moth-orchids – and did I keep them? Don't get restless – I'm coming back to the point. No, I sat beside them a little while having my tea, and saying to myself: "You're a pretty lot, and you do my cupboard honour, but there's a better place awaiting you—" and with that I took them by the hand around to the Catholic church, and I said, "God is what we make Him, and life doesn't seem to be getting any better," and tiptoed out.

'So, I went around the gallery a third time, and I knew that Hindu or no Hindu, I was in on what was wrong with the world – and I said the world's like that poor distressed moll of a Jenny, never knowing which end to put its mittens on, and pecking about like a mystified rook, until this particular night gave her a hoist and set her up at the banquet (where she has been sitting dumbfounded ever since), and Robin the sleeping and troubled, looking amazed. It was more than a boy like me (who am the last woman left in this world, though I am the bearded lady) could bear, and I went into a lather of misery watching them, and thinking of you, and how in the end you'll all be locked together, like the poor beasts that get their antlers mixed and are found dead that way, their heads fattened with a knowledge of each other they never wanted, having had to contemplate each other, head-on and eye to eye, until death; well, that will be you and Jenny and Robin. You, who should have had a thousand children and Robin, who should have been all of them; and Jenny the bird, snatching the oats out of love's droppings – and I went mad, I'm like that. What an autopsy I'll make, with everything all which ways in my bowels! A kidney and a shoe cast of the Roman races; a liver and a long-spent whisper, a gall and a wrack of scolds from Milano, and my heart that will be weeping still when they find my eyes cold, not to mention a thought of Cellini in my crib of bones, thinking how he must have suffered when he knew he could not tell it for ever – (beauty's name spreads too thick). And the lining of my belly, flocked with the locks cut off love in odd places that I've come on, a bird's nest to lay my lost eggs in, and my people as good as they come, as long as they have been coming, down the grim path of "We know not" to "We can't guess why."

'Well, I was thinking of you, a woman at best, and you know what that means? Not much in the morning – all trussed up with pain's bridle. Then I turned my eyes on Jenny, who was turning her eyes looking for trouble, for she was then at that pitch of life that she knew to be her last moment. And do you need the doctor to tell you that that is a bad strange hour for a woman? If all women could have it all at once, you could beat them in flocks like a school of scorpions; but they come eternally, one after the other, and go head foremost into it alone. For men of my kind it isn't so bad, I've never asked better than to see the two ends of my man no matter how I might be dwindling. But for one like Jenny, the poor ruffled bitch, why, God knows, I bled for her, because I knew in an instant the kind of a woman she was, one who had spent all her life rummaging through photographs of the past, searching for the one who would be found leaning sideways with a look as if angels were sliding down her hip – a great love who had been spared a face but who'd been saddled with loins, leaning against a drape of Scotch velvet with a pedestal at the left twined with ivy, a knife in her boot and her groin pouting as if she kept her heart in it. Or searching among old books for the passion that was all renunciation and lung trouble, with flowers at the bosom – that was Jenny – so you can imagine how she trembled when she saw herself going toward fifty without a thing done to make her a tomb-piece, or anything in her past that would get a flower named for her. So I saw her coming forward, stepping lightly and trembling and looking at Robin, saying to me (I'd met her, if you call it meeting a woman when you pound her kidney), "Won't you introduce me?" and my knees knocking together; and my heart as heavy as Adam's off ox, because you are a friend of mine and a good poor thing, God knows, who will never put a stop to anything; you may be knocked down, but you'll crawl on for ever, while there's any use to it, so I said, "Certainly, damn it!" and brought them together. As if Robin hadn't met enough people without me making it worse.'

'Yes,' she said, 'she met every one.'

'Well,' he went on, 'The house was beginning to empty, all the common clay was pouring down the steps talking of the Diva (there's something wrong with any art that makes a woman all bust!) and how she had taken her high L, and all the people looking out of the corner of their eyes to see how their neighbours were dressed, and some of them dropping their cloaks rather low to see the beast in a man snarling up in his neck – and they never guessed that it was me, with both shoulders under cover, that brought the veins to their escorts' temples – and walking high and stately – the pit of my stomach gone black in the darkness that was eating it away for thinking of you, and Robin smiling sideways like a cat with canary feathers to account for, and Jenny tripping beside her so fast that she would get ahead and have to run back with small cries of ambition, saying wistfully, "You must come to my house for late supper."

'God help me, I went! For who will not betray a friend, or, for that matter, himself, for a whisky and soda, caviare and a warm fire – and that brings me to the ride that we took later. As Don Antonio said long ago, "Did'st thou make a night of it?" And was answered (by Claudio), "Yes. Egad! And morning too; for about eight o'clock the next day, slap! They all soused upon their knees, kissed around, burned their commodes, drank my health, broke their glasses and so parted." So Cibber put it, and I put it in Taylor's words: "Did not Periander think fit to lie with his wife Melissa after she had already gone hent to heaven?" Is this not night work of another order also, but night work still? And in another place, as Montaigne says: "Seems it not to be a lunatic humour of the moon that Endymion was by the lady moon lulled to sleep for many months together that she might have her joy of him who stirred not at all except in sleep."

'Well, having picked up a child in transit, a niece of someone Jenny knew, we all went riding down the Champs-Elysées. We went straight as a die over the Pont Neuf, and whirled around into the rue du Cherche-Midi, God forgive us! Where you, weak vessel of love, were lying awake and wondering where, and all the time Jenny doing the deed that was as bad and out of place as that done by Catherine of Russia, and don't deny it, who took old Poniatovsky's throne for a water closet. And suddenly I was glad I was simple and didn't want a thing in the world but what could be had for five francs. And I envied Jenny nothing she had in her house, though I admit I had been sort of casting my eye over a couple of books, which I would have spirited away if they hadn't been bound in calf – for I might steal the mind of Petronius, as well I knew, but never the skin of a calf – for the rest, the place was as full of the wrong thing as you would care to spend your inheritance on – well, I furnished my closet with phenomenal luck at the fair, what with shooting a row of chamber pots and whirling a dozen wheels to the good, and every one about me getting nothing for a thousand francs but a couple of velvet dogs, or dolls that looked as if they had been up all night. And what did I walk home with for less than five francs? A fine frying pan that could coddle six eggs, and a raft of minor objects that one needs in the kitchen – so I looked at Jenny's possessions with scorn in my eye. It may have been all most "unusual", but who wants a toe-nail that is thicker than common? And that thought came to me out of the contemplation of the mad strip of the inappropriate that runs through creation, like my girl friend who married some sort of Adriatic bird who had such thick ones that he had to trim them with a horse file – my mind is so rich that it is always wandering! Now I am back to the time when that groom walked into my life wearing a priest's collar that he had no more right to than I have to a crupper. Well, then the carriages came up with their sweet wilted horses, and Robin went down the steps first, and Jenny tearing after her saying, "Wait! Wait!" as if she were talking to an express on its way into Boston, and dragging her shawl and running, and we all got in – she'd collected some guests who were waiting for her in the house.'

The doctor was embarrassed by Nora's rigid silence; he went on. 'I was leaning forward on my cane as we went down under the trees, holding it with both hands, and the black wagon I was in was being followed by a black wagon, and that by another, and the wheels were turning, and I began saying to myself: The trees are better, and grass is better, and animals are all right and the birds in the air are fine. And everything we do is decent when the mind begins to forget – the design of life; and good when we are forgotten – the design of death. I began to mourn for my spirit, and the spirits of all people who cast a shadow a long way beyond what they are; and for the beasts that walk out of the darkness alone, I began to wail for all the little beasts in their mothers, who would have to step down and begin going decent in the one fur that would last them their time. And I said to myself: For these I would go bang on my knees, but not for her – I wouldn't piss on her if she were on fire! I said, Jenny is so greedy that she wouldn't give her shit to the crows. And then I thought: Oh, the poor bitch, if she were dying, face down in a long pair of black gloves, would I forgive her? And I knew I would forgive her, or anyone making a picture. And then I began looking at the people in that carriage, very carefully raising my eyes so they would not notice anything unusual, and I saw the English girl sitting up there pleased and frightened.

'And then at the child – there was terror in it and it was running away from something grown up; I saw that she was sitting still and she was running, it was in her eyes, and in her chin, drawn down, and her eyes wide open. And then I saw Jenny sitting there shaking, and I said: God, you are no picture! And then, Robin was going forward, and the blood running red, where Jenny had scratched her, and I screamed and thought: "Nora will leave that girl some day; but though those two were buried at opposite ends of the earth, one dog will find them both."'

CHAPTER SIX

Where the Tree Falls

Baron Felix, who had given up his place in the bank, though not his connections with it, had been seen in many countries standing before that country's palace gate, holding his gloved hands before him in the first unconcluded motion of submission; contemplating relics and parts, with a tension in his leg that took the step forward or back a little quicker than his fellow sightseer.

As at one time he had written to the press about this noble or that (and had never seen it in print), as he had sent letters to declining houses and never received an answer, he was now amassing a set of religious speculations that he eventually intended sending to the Pope. The reason for this was, that as time passed it became increasingly evident that his child, if born to anything, had been born to holy decay. Mentally deficient, and emotionally excessive, an addict to death; at ten, barely as tall as a child of six, wearing spectacles, stumbling when he tried to run, with cold hands and anxious face, he followed his father, trembling with an excitement that was a precocious ecstasy. Holding his father's hand he climbed palace and church steps with the tearing swing of the leg necessitated by a measure that had not taken a child into account; staring at paintings and wax reproductions of saints, watching the priests with the quickening of the breath of those in whom concentration must take the place of participation, as in the scar of a wounded animal will be seen the shudder of its recovery.

When Guido had first spoken of wishing to enter the church, Felix had been startled out of himself. He knew that Guido was not like other children, that he would always be too estranged to be argued with; in accepting his son the Baron saw that he must accept a demolition of his own life. The child would obviously never be able to cope with it. The Baron bought his boy a virgin in metal, hanging from a red ribbon, and placed it about his neck, and in doing so, the slight neck, bent to take the ribbon, recalled to him Robin's, as she stood back to him in the antique shop on the Seine.

So Felix began to look into the matter of the church. He searched the face of every priest he saw in the streets; he read litanies and examined chasubles and read the Credo; he inquired into the state of monasteries. He wrote, after much thought, to the Pope, a long disquisition on the state of the cloth. He touched on Franciscan monks and French priests, pointing out that any faith that could, in its profoundest unity, compose two such dissimilar types – one the Roman, shaved and expectant of what seemed, when one looked into his vacantly absorbed face, nothing more glorious than a muscular resurrection; and the other, the French priest, who seemed to be composite of husband and wife in conjunction with original sin, carrying with them good and evil in constantly quantitative ascent and descent, the unhappy spectacle of a single ego come to a several public dissolution, – must be profoundly elastic.

He inquired if this might not be the outcome of the very different confessional states of the two countries. Was it not, he asked, to be taken for granted that the Italian ear must be less confounded because, possibly, it was harking the echo of its past, and the French that of the future? Was it conceivable that the 'confessions' of the two nations could, in the one case, produce that living and expectant coma and, in the other, that worldly, incredible, indecent gluttony? He said that he himself had come to the conclusion that the French, the more secular, were a very porous people. Assuming this, it was then only natural that from listening to a thousand and one lay sins, the priest, upon reaching no riper age than two score, should find it difficult to absolve, the penitent having laid himself open to a peculiar kind of forgiveness; not so much absolution as exigency, for the priest was himself a vessel already filled to overflowing, and gave pardon because he could no longer hold – he signed with the cross, hastily and in stress, being, like a full bladder, embarrassed and in need of immediate privacy. The Franciscan, on the other hand, had still a moment to wait. There was no tangent in his iris, as one who, in blessing is looking for relief.

Felix received no answer. He had expected none. He wrote to clear some doubt in his mind. He knew that in all probability the child would never be 'chosen'. If he were the Baron hoped that it would be Austria, among his own people, and to that end he finally decided to make his home in Vienna.

Before leaving, however, he sought out the doctor. He was not in his lodging. The Baron aimlessly set off toward the square. He saw the small black-clad figure moving toward him. The doctor had been to a funeral and was on his way to the Café de la Mairie du VIᵉ to lift his spirits. The Baron was shocked to observe, in the few seconds before the doctor saw him, that he seemed old, older than his fifty odd years would account for. He moved slowly as if he were dragging water; his knees, which one seldom noticed, because he was usually seated, sagged. His dark shaved chin was lowered as if in a melancholy that had no beginning or end. The Baron hailed him, and instantly the doctor threw off his unobserved self, as one hides, hastily, a secret life. He smiled, drew himself up, raised his hand in greeting, though, as is usual with people when taken unaware, with a touch of defence.

'Where have you been?' he said as he came to a standstill in the middle of the block. 'I haven't seen you for months, and,' he added, 'it's a pity.'

The Baron smiled in return. 'I've been in mental trouble,' he said, walking beside the doctor. 'Are you,' he added, 'engaged for dinner?'

'No,' said the doctor, 'I've just buried an excellent fellow. Don't think you ever met him, a Kabyle, better sort of Arab. They have Roman blood, and can turn pale at a great pinch, which is more than can be said for most, you know,' he added, walking a little sideways, as one does when not knowing where a companion is going. 'Do a bit for a Kabyle, back or front, and they back up on you with a camel or a bag of dates.' He sighed and passed his hand over his chin. 'He was the only one I ever knew who offered me five francs before I could reach for my own. I had it framed in orange blossoms and hung it over the whatnot.'

The Baron was abstracted, but he smiled out of polite-ness. He suggested dining in the Bois. The doctor was only too willing, and at the sudden good news, he made that series of half-gestures of a person taken pleasantly unaware; he half held up his hands – no gloves – he almost touched his breast pocket – a handkerchief; he glanced at his boots, and was grateful for the funeral; he was shined, fairly neat; he touched his tie, stretching his throat muscles.

As they drove through the Bois the doctor went over in his mind what he would order – duck with oranges, no – having eaten on a poor man's purse for so many years, habit had brought him to simple things with garlic. He shivered. He must think of something different. All he could think of was coffee and Grand Marnier, the big tumbler warmed with the hands, like his people warming at the peat fire. 'Yes?' he said, and realized that the Baron had been speaking. The doctor lifted his chin to the night air and listened now with an intensity with which he hoped to reconstruct the sentence.

'Strange, I had never seen the Baronin in this light before,' the Baron was saying, and he crossed his knees. 'If I should try to put it into words, I mean how I did see her, it would be incomprehensible, for the simple reason that I find that I never did have a really clear idea of her at any time. I had an image of her, but that is not the same thing. An image is a stop the mind makes between uncertainties. I had gathered, of course, a good deal from you, and later, after she went away, from others, but this only strengthened my confusion. The more we learn of a person, the less we know. It does not, for instance, help me to know anything of Chartres above the fact that it possesses a cathedral, unless I have lived in Chartres and so keep the relative heights of the cathedral and the lives of its population in proportion. Otherwise it would only confuse me to learn that Jean of that city stood his wife upright in a well; the moment I visualize this, the deed will measure as high as the building; just as children who have a little knowledge of life will draw a man and a barn on the same scale.'

'Your devotion to the past,' observed the doctor, looking at the cab meter with apprehension, 'is perhaps like a child's drawing.'

The Baron nodded. He was troubled. 'My family is preserved because I have it only from the memory of a single woman, my aunt; therefore it is single, clear and unalterable. In this I am fortunate, through this I have a sense of immortality. Our basic idea of eternity is a condition that *cannot vary*. It is the motivation of marriage. No man really wants his freedom. He gets a habit as quickly as possible – it is a form of immortality.'

'And what's more,' said the doctor, 'we heap reproaches on the person who breaks it, saying that in so doing he has broken the image – of our safety.'

The Baron acquiesced. 'This quality of one sole condition, which was so much a part of the Baronin, was what drew me to her; a condition of being that she had not, at that time, even chosen, but a fluid sort of possession which gave me a feeling that I would not only be able to achieve immortality, but be free to choose my own kind.'

'She was always holding God's bag of tricks upside down,' murmured the doctor.

'Yet, if I tell the whole truth,' the Baron continued, 'the very abundance of what then appeared to me to be security, and which was, in reality, the most formless loss, gave me at the same time pleasure and a sense of terrible anxiety, which proved only too legitimate.'

The doctor lit a cigarette.

'I took it,' the Baron went on, 'for acquiescence, thus making my great mistake. She was really like those people who, coming unexpectedly into a room, silence the company because they are looking for someone who is not there.' He knocked on the cab window, got down and paid. As they walked up the gravel path he went on: 'What I particularly wanted to ask you was, why did she marry me? It has placed me in the dark for the rest of my life.'

'Take the case of the horse who knew too much,' said the doctor, 'looking between the branches in the morning, cypress or hemlock. She was in mourning for something taken away from her in a bombardment in the war – by the way she stood, that something lay between her hooves – she stirred no branch, though her hide was a river of sorrow; she was damned to her hocks, where the grass came waving up softly. Her eyelashes were grey-black, like the eyelashes of a nigger, and at her buttocks' soft centre a pulse throbbed like a fiddle.'

The Baron, studying the menu, said, 'The Petherbridge woman called on me.'

'Glittering God,' exclaimed the doctor putting the card down. 'Has it gone as far as that? I shouldn't have thought it.'

'For the first moment,' the Baron continued, 'I had no idea who she was. She had spared no pains to make her toilet rusty and grievous by an arrangement of veils and flat-toned dark material with flowers in it, cut plainly and extremely tight over a very small bust, and from the waist down gathered into bulky folds to conceal, no doubt, the widening parts of a woman well over forty. She seemed hurried. She spoke of you.'

The doctor put the menu on his knee. He raised his dark eyes with the bushy brows erect. 'What did she say?'

The Baron answered, evidently unaware of the tender spot which his words touched: 'Utter nonsense, to the effect that you are seen nearly every day in a certain nunnery, where you bow and pray and get free meals and attend cases which are, well, illegal.'

The Baron looked up. To his surprise he saw that the doctor had 'deteriorated' into that condition in which he had seen him in the street, when he thought himself unobserved.

In a loud voice the doctor said to the waiter, who was within an inch of his mouth: 'Yes, and with oranges, *oranges*!'

The Baron continued hastily: 'She gave me uneasiness because Guido was in the room at the time. She said that she had come to buy a painting – indeed, she offered me a very good price, which I was tempted to take (I've been doing a little dealing in old masters lately) for my stay in Vienna – but, as it turned out, she wanted the portrait of my grandmother, which on no account could I bring myself to part with. She had not been in the room five minutes before I sensed that the picture was an excuse, and that what she really wanted was something else. She began talking about the Baronin almost at once, though she mentioned no name at first, and I did not connect the story with my wife until the end. She said, "She is really quite extraordinary. I don't understand her at all, though I must say I understand her better than other people." She added this with a sort of false eagerness. She went on: "She always lets her pets die. She is so fond of them, and then she neglects them, the way that animals neglect themselves."

'I did not like her to talk about this subject, as Guido is very sensitive to animals, and I could fancy what was going on in his mind; he is not like other children, not cruel, or savage. For this very reason he is called " strange". A child who is mature, in the sense that the heart is mature, is always, I have observed, called deficient.' He gave his order and went on, 'She then changed the subject—'

'Tacking into the wind like a barge.'

'Well, yes, to a story about a little girl she had staying with her (she called her Sylvia); the Baronin was also staying with her at the time, though I did not know that the young woman in question was the Baronin until later – well anyway it appears that this little girl Sylvia had "fallen in love" with the Baronin, and that she, the Baronin, kept waking her up all through the night to ask her if she "loved her".

'During the holidays, while the child was away, Pether-bridge became "anxious" – that is the way she put it – as to whether or not the "young lady had a heart".'

'And brought the child back to prove it?' interpolated the doctor, casting an eye over the fashionable crowd beginning to fill the room.

'Exactly,' said the Baron, ordering wine. 'I made an exclamation, and she said quickly: "You can't blame me, you can't accuse me of using a child for my own ends!" Well, what else does it come to?'

'That woman,' the doctor said, settling himself more comfortably in his chair, 'would use the third-rising of a corpse for her ends. Though,' he added, 'I must admit she is very generous with money.'

The Baron winced. 'So I gathered from her over-large bid for the portrait. Well, she went on to say that, when they met, the Baronin had so obviously forgotten all about her, that the child was "ashamed". She said "shame went all over her". She was already at the door when she spoke the last sentence. In fact, she conducted the whole scene as though my room were a stage that had been marked out, and at this point she must read her final lines.'

'"Robin," she said, "Baronin Robin Volkbein, I wonder if she could be a relative."'

'For a whole minute I couldn't move. When I turned around I saw that Guido was ill. I took him in my arms and spoke to him in German. He had often put questions to me about his mother and I had managed always to direct his mind to expect her.'

The doctor turned to the Baron with one of his sudden illuminations. 'Exactly right. With Guido, you are in the presence of the "maladjusted". Wait! I am not using that word in the derogatory sense at all, in fact my great virtue is that I never use the derogatory in the usual sense. Pity is an intrusion when in the presence of a person who is a new position in an old account – which is your son. You can only pity those limited to their generation. Pity is timely, and dies with the person; a pitiable man is his own last tie. You have treated Guido well.'

The Baron paused, his knife bent down. He looked up. 'Do you know, doctor, I find the thought of my son's possible death at an early age a sort of dire happiness, because his death is the most awful, the most fearful thing that could befall me. The unendurable is the beginning of the curve of joy. I have become entangled in the shadow of a vast apprehension which is my son; he is the central point toward which life and death are spinning, the meeting of which my final design will be composed.'

'And Robin?' the doctor asked.

'She is with me in Guido, they are inseparable, and this time,' the Baron said, catching his monocle, 'with her full consent.' He leaned down and picked up his napkin. 'The Baronin,' he continued, 'always seemed to be looking for someone to tell her that she was innocent. Guido is very like her, except that he has his innocence. The Baronin was always searching in the wrong direction, until she met Nora Flood, who seemed, from what little I knew of her, to be a very honest woman, at least by intention.'

'There are some people,' he went on, 'who must get permission to live, and if the Baronin finds no one to give her that permission, she will make an innocence for herself; a fearful sort of primitive innocence. It may be considered, "depraved" by our generation, but our generation does not know everything.' He smiled. 'For instance Guido, how many will realize his value? One's life is peculiarly one's own when one has invented it.'

The doctor wiped his mouth. 'In the acceptance of depravity the sense of the past is most fully captured. What is a ruin but Time easing itself of endurance? Corruption is the Age of Time. It is the body and the blood of ecstasy, religion and love. Ah, yes,' the doctor added, 'we do not "climb" to heights, we are eaten away to them, and then conformity, neatness, ceases to entertain us. Man is born as he dies, rebuking cleanliness; and there is its middle condition, the slovenliness that is usually an accompaniment of the "attractive" body, a sort of earth on which love feeds.'

'That is true,' Felix said with eagerness. 'The Baronin had an undefinable disorder, a sort of "odour of memory", like a person who has come from some place that we have forgotten and would give our life to recall.'

The doctor reached out for the bread. 'So the reason for our cleanliness becomes apparent; cleanliness is a form of apprehension; our faulty racial memory is fathered by fear. Destiny and history are untidy; we fear memory of that disorder. Robin did not.'

'No,' Felix said in a low voice. 'She did not.'

'The almost fossilized state of our recollection is attested to by our murderers and those who read every detail of crime with a passionate and hot interest,' the doctor continued. 'It is only by such extreme measures that the average man can remember something long ago; truly, not that he remembers, but that crime itself is the door to an accumulation, a way to lay hands on the shudder of a past that is still vibrating.'

The Baron was silent a moment. Then he said: 'Yes,

something of this rigour was in the Baronin, in its first faint degree; it was in her walk, in the way she wore her clothes, in her silence, as if speech were heavy and unclarified. There was in her every movement a slight drag, as if the past were a web about her, as there is a web of time about a very old building. There is a sensible weight in the air around a thirteenth-century edifice,' he said with a touch of pomposity, 'that is unlike the light air about a new structure; the new building seems to repulse it, the old to gather it. So about the Baronin there was a density, not of age, but of youth. It perhaps accounts for my attraction to her.'

'Animals find their way about largely by the keenness of their nose,' said the doctor. 'We have lost ours in order not to be one of them, and what have we in its place? A tension in the spirit which is the contraction of freedom. But,' he ended, 'all dreadful events are of profit.'

Felix ate in silence for a moment, then point-blank he turned to the doctor with a question. 'You know my preoccupation; is my son's better?'

The doctor, as he grew older, in answering a question seemed, as old people do, to be speaking more and more to himself, and, when troubled, he seemed to grow smaller. He said: 'Seek no further for calamity; you have it in your son. After all, calamity is what we are all seeking. You have found it. A man is whole only when he takes into account his shadow as well as himself – and what is a man's shadow but his upright astonishment? Guido is the shadow of your anxiety, and Guido's shadow is God's.'

Felix said: 'Guido also loves women of history.'

'Mary's shadow!' said the doctor.

Felix turned. His monocle shone sharp and bright along its edge. 'People say that he is not sound of mind. What do you say?'

'I say that a mind like his may be more apt than yours and mine – he is not made secure by habit – in that there is always hope.'

Felix said under his breath: 'He does not grow up.'

Matthew answered: 'The excess of his sensibilities may preclude his mind. His sanity is an unknown room: a known room is always smaller than an unknown. If I were you,' the doctor continued, 'I would carry that boy's mind like a bowl picked up in the dark; you do not know what's in it. He feeds on odd remnants that we have not priced; he eats a sleep that is not our sleep. There is more in sickness than the name of that sickness. In the average person is the peculiar that has been scuttled, and in the peculiar the ordinary that has been sunk; people always fear what requires watching.'

Felix ordered a *fine*. The doctor smiled. 'I said you would come to it,' he said, and emptied his own glass at a gulp.

'I know,' Felix answered, 'but I did not understand. I though you meant something else.'

'What?'

Felix paused, turning the small glass around in his trembling hand. 'I thought,' he said, 'that you meant that I would give up.'

The doctor lowered his eyes. 'Perhaps that is what I meant – but sometimes I am mistaken.' He looked at Felix from under his heavy brows. 'Man was born damned and innocent from the start, and wretchedly – as he must – on those two themes – whistles his tune.'

The Baron leaned forward. He said, in a low voice, 'Was the Baronin damned?'

The doctor deliberated for a second, knowing what Felix had hidden in his question. 'Guido is not damned,' he said, and the Baron turned away quickly. 'Guido,' the doctor went on, 'is blessed – he is peace of mind – he is what you have always been looking for – Aristocracy,' he said smiling, 'is a condition in the mind of the people when they try to think of something else and better – funny,' he added sharply, 'that a man never knows when he has found what he has always been looking for.'

'And the Baronin,' Felix said, 'do you ever hear from her?'

'She is in America now, but of course you know that. Yes, she writes, now and again, not to me – God forbid – to others.'

'What does she say?' the Baron said, trying not to show his emotion.

'She says,' the doctor answered, "Remember me." Probably because she has difficulty in remembering herself.'

The Baron caught his monocle. 'Altamonte, who has been in America, tells me that she seemed "estranged". Once,' he said, pinching his monocle into place, 'I wanted, as you, who are aware of everything, know, to go behind the scenes, back-stage as it were, to our present condition, to find, if I could, the secret of time; good, perhaps that that is an impossible ambition for the sane mind. One has, I am now certain, to be a little mad to see into the past or the future, to be a little abridged of life to know life, the obscure life – darkly seen, the condition my son lives in; it may also be the errand on which the Baronin is going.'

Taking out his handkerchief, the Baron removed his monocle, wiping it carefully.

Carrying a pocket full of medicines, and a little flask of oil for the chapping hands of his son, Felix rode into Vienna, the child beside him; Frau Mann, opulent and gay, opposite, holding a rug for the boy's feet. Felix drank heavily now, and to hide the red that flushed his cheeks he had grown a beard ending in two forked points on his chin. In the matter of drink, Frau Mann was now no bad second. Many cafés saw this odd trio, the child in the midst wearing heavy lenses that made his eyes drift forward, sitting erect, his neck holding his head at attention, watching his father's coins roll, as the night drew out, farther and farther across the floor and under the feet of the musicians as Felix called for military music, for *Wacht am Rhein*, for *Morgenrot*, for Wagner; his monocle dimmed by the heat of the room, perfectly correct and drunk, trying not to look for what he had always sought, the son of a once great house; his eyes either gazing at the ceiling or lowered where his hand, on the table, struck thumb and little finger against the wood in rhythm with the music, as if he were playing only the two important notes of an octave, the low and the high; or nodding his head and smiling at his child, as mechanical toys nod to the touch of an infant's hand, Guido pressing his own hand against his stomach where, beneath his shirt, he could feel the medallion against his flesh, Frau Mann gripping her beer mug firmly, laughing and talking loudly.

One evening, seated in his favourite café on the Ring, Felix on entering had seen instantly, but refused to admit it to himself, a tall man in the corner who, he was sure, was the Grand Duke Alexander of Russia, cousin and brother-in-law of the late Czar Nicholas – and toward whom in the early part of the evening he steadfastly refused to look. But as the clock hands pointed twelve, Felix (with the abandon of what a mad man knows to be his one hope of escape, disproof of his own madness) could not keep his eyes away, and as they arose to go, his cheeks now drained of colour, the points of his beard bent sharply down with the stiffening back of his chin, he turned and made a slight bow, his head in his confusion making a complete half-swing, as an animal will turn its head away from a human, as if in mortal shame.

He stumbled as he got into his carriage. 'Come,' he said, taking the child's fingers in his own. 'You are cold.' He poured a few drops of oil, and began rubbing Guido's hands.

CHAPTER SEVEN

Go Down, Matthew

'Can't you be quiet now?' the doctor said. He had come in late one afternoon to find Nora writing a letter. 'Can't you be done now, can't you give up? Now be still, now that you know what the world is about, knowing it's about nothing?' He took his hat and coat off without being asked, placing his umbrella in a corner. He came forward into the room. 'And me who seem curious because no one has seen me for a million years, and now I'm seen! Is there such extraordinary need of misery to make beauty? Let go Hell; and your fall will be broken by the roof of Heaven.' He eyed the tea-tray and, seeing that the tea-pot had long since become cold, poured himself a generous port. He threw himself into a chair and added more softly, as Nora turned away from her letter, 'In the far reaches of India there is a man being still beneath a tree. Why not rest? Why not put the pen away? Isn't it bitter enough for Robin that she is lost somewhere without receiving mail? And Jenny, what of her now? Taken to drink and appropriating Robin's mind with vulgar inaccuracy, like those eighty-two plaster virgins she bought because Robin had one good one; when you laugh at the eighty-two standing in a row, Jenny runs to the wall, back to the picture of her mother, and stands there between two tortures – the past that she can't share, and the present that she can't copy. What of her now? Looking at her quarters with harrowing, indelicate cries; burying her middle at both ends, searching the world for the path back to what she wanted once and long ago! The memory past, and only by a coincidence, a wind, the flutter of a leaf, a surge of tremendous recollection goes through her, and swooning she knows it gone. Cannot a beastly thing be analogous to a fine thing, if both are apprehensions? Love of two things often makes one thing right. Think of the fish racing the sea, their love of air and water turning them like wheels, their tails and teeth biting the water, their spines curved round the air. Is that not Jenny? She who could not encompass anything whole, but only with her teeth and tail, and the spine on her sprung up. Oh, for God's sake! Can't you rest now?'

'If I don't write to her, what am I to do? I can't sit here for ever – thinking!'

'*Terra damnata et maledicta!*' exclaimed the doctor, banging his fist down. 'My uncle Octavius, the trout-tickler of Itchen, was better, he ate his fish when he caught it! But you, you must unspin fate, go back to find Robin! That's what you are going to do. In your chair should have been set the Holy Stone, to say yes to your yes, no to your no; instead it's lost in Westminster Abbey, and if I could have stopped Brech on his way with it into Ireland and have whispered in his ear I would have said, "Wait" (though it was seven hundred years BC); it might have been passed around. It might have stopped you, but no, you are always writing to Robin. Nothing will curb it. You've made her a legend and set before her head the Eternal Light, and you'll keep to it even if it does cost her the tearing open of a million envelopes to her end. How do you know what sleep you raise her from? What words she must say to annul the postman's whistle to another girl rising up on a wild elbow? Can't you let any of us loose? Don't you know your holding on is her only happiness and so her sole misery. You write and weep and think and plot, and all the time what is Robin doing? Chucking Jack Straws, or sitting on the floor playing soldiers; so don't cry to me, who have no one to write to, and only taking in a little light laundry known as the Wash of the World. Dig a hole, drop me in! Not at all. St Matthew's Passion by Bach I'll be. Everything can be used in a lifetime, I've discovered that.'

'I've got to write to her,' Nora said. 'I've got to.'

'No man knows it as I know it, I who am the god of darkness. Very well, but know the worst, then. What of Felix and his son Guido, that sick lamenting, fevered child? Death in the weather is a tonic to him. Like all the new young his sole provision for old age is hope of an early death. What spirits answer him who will never come to man's estate? The poor shattered eagerness. So, I say, was Robin purposely unspun? Was Jenny a sitting bitch for fun? Who knows what knives hash her apart? Can't you rest now, lay down the pen? Oh, *papelero*, have I not summed up my time! I shall rest myself some day by the brim of Saxon-les-Bains and drink it dry, or go to pieces in Hamburg at the gambling table, or end up like Madame de Staël – with an affinity for Germany. To all kinds of ends I'll come. Ah yes, with a crupper of maiden's hair to keep my soul in place, and in my vanguard a dove especially feathered to keep to my wind, as I ride that grim horse with ample glue in every hoof to post up my deeds when I'm dropped in and sealed with earth. In time everything is possible and in space everything forgivable; life is but the intermediary vice. There is eternity to blush in. Life laid end to end is what brings on flux in the clergy – can't you rest now, put down the pen? Oh, the poor worms that never arrive! Some strangely connived angel pray for us! We shall not encompass it – the defunctive murmur in the cardiac nerve has given us all our gait. And Robin? I know where your mind is! She, the eternal momentary – Robin who was always the second person singular. Well,' he said with violence, 'lie weeping with a sword in your hand! Haven't I eaten a book too? Like the angels and prophets? And wasn't it a bitter book to eat? The archives of my case against the law, snatched up and out of the tale-telling files by my high important friend. And didn't I eat a page and tear a page and stamp on others and flay some and toss some into the toilet for relief's sake – then think of Jenny without a comma to eat, and Robin with nothing but a pet name – your pet name to sustain her; for pet names are a guard against loss, like primitive music. But does that sum her up? Is even the end of us an account? No, don't answer, I know that even the memory has weight. Once in the war I saw a dead horse that had been lying long against the ground. Time and the birds, and its own last concentration had removed the body a great way from the head. As I looked upon that head, my memory weighed for the lost body; and because of that missing quantity even heavier hung that head along the ground. So love, when it has gone, taking time with it, leaves a memory of its weight.'

She said: 'She is myself. What am I to do?'

'Make birds' nests with your teeth, that would be better,' he said angrily, 'like my English girl friend. The birds liked them so well that they stopped making their own (does that sound like any nest you have made for any bird, and so broken it of its fate?). In the spring they form a queue by her bedroom window and stand waiting their turn, holding on to their eggs as hard as they can until she gets around to them, strutting up and down on the ledge, the eyes in their feathers a quick shine and sting, whipped with impatience, like a man waiting at a toilet door for someone inside who had decided to read *The Decline and Fall of the Roman Empire*. And then think of Robin who never could provide for her life except in you. Oh, well,' he said under his breath, ' "happy are they whom privacy makes innocent". '

Nora turned around, and speaking in a voice that she tried to make steady said: 'Once, when she was sleeping, I wanted her to die. Now, that would stop nothing.'

The doctor, nodding, straightened his tie with two fingers. 'The number of our days is not check rein enough to look upon the death of our love. While living we knew her too well, and never understood, for then our next gesture permitted our next misunderstanding. But death is intimacy walking backward. We are crazed with grief when she, who once permitted us, leaves to us the only recollection. We shed tears of bankruptcy then. So it's well she didn't.' He sighed. 'You are still in trouble – I thought you had put yourself outside of it. I might have known better, nothing is what everybody wants, the world runs on that law. Personally, if I could, I would instigate Meat-Axe Day, and out of the goodness of my heart I would whack your head off along with a couple of others. Every man should be allowed one day and a hatchet just to ease his heart.'

She said: 'What will happen now, to me and to her?'

'Nothing,' the doctor answered, 'as always. We all go down in battle, but we all come home.'

She said: 'I can only find her again in my sleep or in her death; in both she has forgotten me.'

'Listen,' the doctor said, putting down his glass. 'My war brought me many things; let yours bring you as much. Life is not to be told, call it as loud as you like, it will not tell itself. No one will be much or little except in someone else's mind, so be careful of the minds you get into, and remember Lady Macbeth, who had her mind in her hand. We can't all be as safe as that.'

Nora got up nervously and began walking. 'I'm so miserable, Matthew, I don't know how to talk, and I've got to. I've got to talk to somebody. I can't live this way.' She pressed her hands together, and without looking at the doctor, went on walking.

'Have you any more port?' he inquired, putting the empty bottle down. Mechanically, Nora brought him a second decanter. He took the stopper out, held it to his nose a moment, then poured himself a glass.

'You are,' he said, testing the wine between his lower lip and teeth, 'experiencing the inbreeding of pain. Most of us do not dare it. We wed a stranger, and so "solve" our problem. But when you inbreed with suffering (which is merely to say that you have caught every disease and so pardoned your flesh) you are destroyed back to your structure as an old master disappears beneath the knife of the scientist who would know how it was painted. Death I imagine will be pardoned by the same identification; we all carry about with us the house of death, the skeleton, but unlike the turtle our safety is inside, our danger out. Time is a great conference planning our end, and youth is only the past putting a leg forward. Ah, to be able to hold on to suffering, but to let the spirit loose! And speaking of being destroyed, allow me to illustrate by telling you of one dark night in London, when I was hurrying along, my hands before me, praying I'd get home and into bed and wake up in the morning without finding my hands on my hips. So I started for London Bridge – all this was a long time ago, and I'd better be careful or one of these days I'll tell a story that will give up my age.

'Well, I went off under London Bridge and what should I see? A Tuppeny Upright! And do you know what a Tuppeny Upright might be? A Tuppeny is an old-time girl, and London Bridge is her last stand, as the last stand for a *grue* is Marseilles, if she doesn't happen to have enough pocket money to get to Singapore. For tuppence, an upright is all anyone can expect. They used to walk along slowly, all ruffles and rags, with big terror hats on them, a pin stuck over the eye and slap up through the crown, half their shadows on the ground and the other half crawling along the wall beside them; ladies of the *haute* sewer taking their last stroll, sauntering on their last Rotten Row, going slowly along in the dark, holding up their badgered flounces, or standing still, silent and as indifferent as the dead, as if they were thinking of better days, or waiting for something that they had been promised when they were little girls; their poor damned dresses hiked up and falling away over the rump, all gathers and braid, like a Crusader's mount, with all the trappings gone sideways with misery.'

While the doctor had been speaking Nora had stopped, as if he had got her attention for the first time.

'And once Father Lucas said to me, "Be simple, Matthew, life is a simple book, and an open book, read and be simple as the beasts in the field; just being miserable isn't enough – you have got to know how." So I got to thinking and I said to myself, "This is a terrible thing that Father Lucas has put on me – be simple like the beasts and yet think and harm nobody." I began walking then. It had begun to snow and the night was down. I went toward the Ile, because I could see the lights in the show-windows of Our Lady and all the children in the dark with the tapers twinkling, saying their prayers softly with that small breath that comes off little lungs, whispering fatally about nothing, which is the way children say their prayers. Then I said, "Matthew, tonight you must find a small church where there are no people where you can be alone like an animal, and yet think." So I turned off and went down until I came to St Merri and went forward and there I was. All the candles were burning steadily for the troubles that people had entrusted to them and I was almost alone, only in a far corner an old peasant woman saying her beads.

'So I walked straight up to the box for the souls in Purgatory, just to show that I was a true sinner, in case there happened to be a Protestant about. I was trying to think which of my hands was the more blessed, because there's a box in the Raspail that says the hand you give with to the Little Sisters of the Poor, that will be blessed all day. I gave it up, hoping it was my right hand. Kneeling in a dark corner, bending my head over and down, I spoke to Tiny O'Toole, because it was his turn, I had tried everything else. There was nothing for it this time but to make him face the mystery so it could see him clear as it saw me. So then I whispered, "What is this thing, Lord?" And I began to cry; the tears went like rain goes down on the world, without touching the face of Heaven. Suddenly I realized that it was the first time in my life my tears were strange to me, because they just went straight forward out of my eyes; I was crying because I had to embarrass Tiny like that for the good it might do to him.

'I was crying and striking my left hand against the prie-Dieu, and all the while Tiny O'Toole was lying in a swoon. I said, "I have tried to seek, and I only find." I said, "It is I, my Lord, who know there's beauty in any permanent mistakes like me. Haven't I said it so? But," I says "I'm not able to stay permanent unless you help me, O Book of Concealment! *C'est le plaisir qui me bouleverse!* The roaring lion goes forth, seeking his own fury! So tell me, what is permanent of me, me or him?" And there I was in the empty, almost empty church, all the people's troubles flickering in little lights all over the place. And I said, "This would be a fine world, Lord, if you could get everybody out of it." And there I was holding Tiny, bending over and crying, asking the question until I forgot, and went on crying, and I put Tiny away then, like a ruined bird, and went out of the place and walked looking at the stars that were twinkling, and I said, "Have I been simple like an animal, God, or have I been thinking?"'

She smiled. 'Sometimes I don't know why I talk to you. You're so like a child; then again I know well enough.'

'Speaking of children – and thanks for the compliment – take for instance the case of Don Anticolo, the young tenor from Beirut – he dipped down into his pelvis for his Wagner, and plunged to his breast pit for his Verdi – he'd sung himself once and a half round the world, a widower with a small son, scarcely ten by the clock when, presto – the boy was bitten by a rat while swimming in Venezia and this brought on a fever. His father would come in and take hold of him every ten minutes (or was it every half-hour?) to see if he was less hot, or hotter. His daddy was demented with grief and fear, but did he leave his bedside for a moment? He did, because, though the son was sick, the fleet was in. But being a father, he prayed as he drank the champagne; and he wished his son alive as he chucked over the compass and invited the crew home, bow and sprit. But when he got home the little son lay dead. The young tenor burst into tears and burned him and had the ashes put into a zinc box no bigger than a doll's crate and held ceremony over him, twelve sailors all in blue standing about the deal table, a glass in their hands, sorrow in their sea-turned eye slanting under lids thinned by the horizon, as the distracted father and singer tossed the little zinc box down upon the table crying: 'This, gentlemen, is my babe, this, lads, my son, my sailors, my boy!" and at that, running to the box and catching it up and dashing it down again, repeating and weeping, "My son, my baby, my boy!" with trembling fingers nudging the box now here now there about the table, until it went up and down its length a dozen times; the father behind it, following it, touching it, weeping and crying like a dog who noses a bird that has, for some strange reason, no more movement.'

The doctor stood up, then sat down again. 'Yes, oh, God, Robin was beautiful. I don't like her, but I have to admit that much: sort of fluid blue under her skin, as if the hide of time had been stripped from her, and with it, all transactions with knowledge. A sort of first position in attention; a face that will age only under the blows of perpetual childhood. The temples like those of young beasts cutting horns, as if they were sleeping eyes. And that look on a face we follow like a witch-fire. Sorcerers know the power of horns; meet a horn where you like and you know you have been identified. You could fall over a thousand human skulls without the same trepidation. And do old duchesses know it also! Have you ever seen them go into a large assembly of any sort, be it opera or bezique, without feathers, flowers, sprigs of oat, or some other gadget nodding above their temples!'

She had not heard him. 'Every hour is my last, and,' she said desperately, 'one can't live one's last hour all one's life!'

He grinned. 'Even the contemplative life is only an effort, Nora my dear, to hide the body so the feet won't stick out.

Ah,' he added, 'to be an animal, born at the opening of the eye, going only forward, and, at the end of day, shutting out memory with the dropping of the lid.'

'Time isn't long enough,' she said, striking the table. 'It isn't long enough to live down her nights. God,' she cried, 'what is love? Man seeking his own head? The human head, so rented by misery that even the teeth weigh! She couldn't tell me the truth, because she had never planned it; her life was a continual accident, and how can you be prepared for that? Everything we can't bear in this world, some day we find in one person, and love it all at once. A strong sense of identity gives man an idea he can do no wrong; too little accomplishes the same. Some natures cannot appreciate, only regret. Will Robin *only* regret?' She stopped abruptly, gripping the back of the chair. 'Perhaps not,' she said, 'for even her memory wearied her.' Then she said with the violence of misery, 'There's something evil in me, that loves evil and degradation – purity's black backside! That loves honesty with a horrid love; or why have I always gone seeking it at the liar's door?'

'Look here,' said the doctor. 'Do you know what has made me the greatest liar this side of the moon, telling my stories to people like you, to take the mortal agony out of their guts, and to stop them from rolling about, and drawing up their feet, and screaming, with their eyes staring over their knuckles with misery which they are trying to keep off, saying, "Say something, doctor, for the love of God!" And me talking away like mad. Well that, and nothing else, has made me the liar I am.

'Suppose your heart were five feet across in any place, would you break it for a heart no bigger than a mouse's mute? Would you hurl yourself into any body of water, in the size you now are, for any woman that you had to look for with a magnifying glass, or any boy if he was as high as the Eiffel Tower or did droppings like a fly? No, we all love in sizes, yet we all cry out in tiny voices to the great booming God, the older we get. Growing old is just a matter of throwing life away back; so you finally forgive even those that you have not begun to forget. It is that indifference which gives you your courage, which to tell the truth is no courage at all. There is no truth, and you have set it between you; you have been unwise enough to make a formula; you have dressed the unknowable in the garments of the known.'

'Man,' she said, her eyelids quivering, 'conditioning himself to fear, made God; as the prehistoric, conditioning itself to hope, made man – the cooling of the earth, the receding of the sea. And I, who want power, chose a girl who resembles a boy.'

'Exactly,' said the doctor. 'You never loved anyone before, and you'll never love anyone again, as you love Robin. Very well – what is this love we have for the invert, boy or girl? It was they who were spoken of in every romance that we ever read. The girl lost, what is she but the Prince found? The Prince on the white horse that we have always been seeking. And the pretty lad who is a girl, what but the prince-princess in point lace – neither one and half the other, the painting on the fan! We love them for that reason. We were impaled in our childhood upon them as they rode through our primers, the sweetest lie of all, now come to be in boy or girl, for in the girl it is the prince, and in the boy it is the girl that makes a prince a prince – and not a man. They go far back in our lost distance where what we never had stands waiting; it was inevitable that we should come upon them, for our miscalculated longing has created them. They are our answer to what our grandmothers were told love was, and what it never came to be; they, the living lie of our centuries. When a long lie comes up, sometimes it is a beauty; when it drops into dissolution, into drugs and drink, into disease and death, it has at once a singular and terrible attraction. A man can resent and avoid evil on his own plane, but when it is the thin blown edge of his reverie, he takes it to his heart, as one takes to one's heart the dark misery of the close nightmare, born and slain of the particular mind; so that if one of them were dying of the pox, one would will to die of it too, with two feelings, terror and joy, welded somewhere back again into a formless sea where a swan (would it be ourselves, or her or him, or a mystery of all) sinks crying.

'Love is death, come upon with passion; I know that is why love is wisdom. I love her as one condemned to it.'

'Oh, Widow Lazarus! Arisen from your dead! Oh, lunatic humour of the moon! Behold this fearful tree, on which sits singing the drearful bird – *Turdus musicus*, or European singing thrush; sitting and singing the refrain – all in the tear-wet night – and it starts out *largo*, but it ends like *I Hear You Calling Me*, or *Kiss Me Again*, gone wild. And Diane, where is she? Diane of Ephesus in the Greek Gardens, singing and shaken in every bosom; and Rack and Ruin, the dogs of the Vatican, running up and down the papal esplanade and out into the Ramblar with roses in their tails to keep off care. Don't I know it all! Do you think that I, the Old Woman who lives in the closet, do not know that every child, no matter what its day, is born prehistorically and that even the wrong thought has caused the human mind incredible effort? Bend down the tree of knowledge and you'll unroost a strange bird. Suffering may be composed wickedly and of an inferior writhing. Rage and inaccuracy howl and blow the bone, for, contrary to all opinion, all suffering does *not* purify – begging everybody's pardon, which is called everybody's know. It moils and blathers some to perjury; the peritoneum boils and brings on common and cheap praying a great way sunk in pointless agony.'

'Jenny,' she said.

'It rots her sleep – Jenny is one of those who nip like a bird and void like an ox – the poor and lightly damned! That can be a torture also. None of us suffers as much as we should, or loves as much as we say. Love is the first lie; wisdom the last. Don't I know that the only way to know evil is through truth? The evil and the good know themselves only by giving up their secret face to face. The true good who meets the true evil (Holy Mother of Mercy! Are there any such?) learns for the first time how to accept neither; the face of the one tells the face of the other the half of the story that both forgot.'

'To be utterly innocent,' he went on, 'would be to be utterly unknown, particularly to oneself.'

'Sometimes Robin seemed to return to me,' Nora said unheeding, 'for sleep and safety, but,' she added bitterly, 'she always went out again.'

The doctor lit a cigarette; lifting his chin he blew the smoke high. 'To treat her lovers to the great passionate indifference. Say,' he exclaimed, bringing his chin down. 'Dawn, of course, dawn! That's when she came back frightened. At that hour the citizen of the night balances on a thread that is running thin.'

'Only the impossible lasts forever; with time, it is made accessible. Robin's love and mine was always impossible, and loving each other, we no longer love. Yet we love each other like death.'

'Um,' murmured the doctor, 'beat life like a dinner bell

yet there is one hour that won't ring – the hour of disentanglement. Oh well,' he sighed, 'everyman dies finally of that poison known as the-heart-in-the-mouth. Yours is in your hand. Put it back. The eater of it will get a taste for you; in the end his muzzle will be heard barking among your ribs. I'm no exception, God knows, I'm the last of my line, the fine hair-line of least resistance. It's a gruesome thing that man learns only by what he has between the one leg and the other! Oh, that short dangle! We corrupt mortality by its industry. You never know which one of your ends it is that is going to be the part you can't take your mind off.'

'If only you could take my mind off, Matthew – now, in this house that I took that Robin's mind and mine might go together. Surprising, isn't it, I'm happier when I'm alone now, without her, because when she was here with me, in this house, I had to watch her wanting to go and yet to stay. How much of our life do we put into a life that we may be damned? Then she was back stumbling through the house again, listening for a footstep in the court, for a way to leave and not to go, trying to absorb, with the intensity of her ear, any sound that would have made me suspicious, yet hoping I would break my heart in safety; she needed that assurance. Matthew, was it a sin that I believed her?'

'Of course, it made her life wrong.'

'But when I didn't believe her any more, after the night I came to see you; that I have to think of all the time, I don't dare to stop, for fear of the moment it will come back again.'

'Remorse,' said the doctor, 'sitting heavy, like the arse of a bull – you had the conceit of "honesty" to keep that arse from cracking your heart; but what did she have? Only your faith in her – then you took that faith away! You should have kept it always, seeing that it was a myth; no myth is safely broken. Ah, the weakness of the strong! The trouble with you is, you are not just a myth-maker, you are also a destroyer, you made a beautiful fable, then put Voltaire to bed with it; ah, the 'Dead March' in *Saul*!

Nora said, as if she had not been interrupted – 'Because after that night, I went to see Jenny. I remember the stairs. They were of brown wood, and the hall was ugly and dark, and her apartment depressing. No one would have known that she had money. The walls had mustard-coloured paper on them as far as the salon, and something hideous in red and green and black in the hall, and away at the end, a bedroom facing the hall door, with a double-bed. Sitting up against the pillow was a doll. Robin had given me a doll. I knew then, before I asked, that this was the right house, before I said, "You are Robin's mistress, aren't you?" That poor shuddering creature had pelvic bones I could see flying through her dress. I wanted to lean forward and laugh with terror. She was sitting there doubled up with surprise, her raven's bill coming up saying, "Yes." Then I looked up and there on the wall was the photograph of Robin when she was a baby (the one that she had told me was lost).

'She went to pieces; she fell forward on my lap. At her next words I saw that I was not a danger to her, but someone who might understand her torture. In great agitation she said, "I went out this afternoon, I didn't think she would call me, because you had been away to the country, Robin said, and would be back this evening and so she would have to stay home with you, because you had been so good to her always; though God knows I under-stand there is nothing between you any longer, that you are 'just good friends'; she has explained that – still, I nearly went mad when I found that she had been here and I was out. She has told me often enough, 'Don't leave the house, because I don't know exactly when I am going to be able to get away, because I can't hurt Nora.'"' Nora's voice broke. She went on.

'Then Jenny said, "What are you going to do? What do you want me to do?" I knew all the time that she could do nothing but what she wanted to do, and that whatever it was, she was a liar, no matter what truth she was telling. I was dead. I felt stronger then, and I said, yes I would have a drink. She poured out two, knocking the bottle against the glass and spilling the liquor on the dark ugly carpet. I kept thinking, what else is it that is hurting me; then I knew – the doll; the doll in there on the bed.' Nora sat down, facing the doctor. 'We give death to a child when we give it a doll – it's the effigy and the shroud; when a woman gives it to a woman, it is the life they cannot have, it is their child, sacred and profane; so when I saw that other doll –' Nora could not go on. She began to cry. 'What part of monstrosity am I that I am always crying at its side!

'When I got home Robin had been waiting, knowing, because I was late, that something was wrong. I said, "It is over – I can't go on. You have always lied to me, and you have denied me to her. I can't stand it any more."

'She stood up then, and went into the hall. She jerked her coat off the hook and I said, "Have you nothing to say to me?" She turned her face to me. It was like something once beautiful found in a river – and flung herself out of the door.'

'And you were crying,' the doctor said, nodding. 'You went about the house like someone sunken under lightness. You were ruined and you kept striking your hands together, laughing crazily and singing a little and putting your hands over your face. Stage-tricks have been taken from life, so finding yourself employing them you were confused with a sense of shame. When you went out looking for someone to go mad with, they said, "For God's sake look at Nora!" For the demolishing of a great ruin is always a fine and terrifying spectacle. Why is it that you want to talk to me? Because I'm the other woman that God forgot.'

'There's nothing to go by, Matthew,' she said. 'You do not know which way to go. A man is another person – a woman is yourself, caught as you turn in panic; on her mouth you kiss your own. If she is taken you cry that you have been robbed of yourself. God laughs at me; but his laughter is my love.'

'You have died and arisen for love,' said Matthew. 'But unlike the ass, returning from the market you are always carrying the same load. Oh, for God's sweet sake, didn't she ever disgust you! Weren't you sometimes pleased that you had the night to yourself, wishing, when she did come home, that it was never?'

'Never, and always; I was frightened she would be gentle again. That,' she said, 'that's an awful fear. Fear of the moment when she would turn her words, making them something between us that nobody else could possibly share – and she would say, "You have got to stay with me or I can't live." Yet one night she ran behind me in the Montparnasse quarter, where I had gone looking for her because someone had called me, saying, she was sick and couldn't get home (I had stopped going out with her because I couldn't bear to see the "evidence of my eyes"); running behind me for blocks saying, with a furious panting breath, "You are a devil! You make everything dirty!" (I had tried to take someone's hands off her. They always put hands on her when she was drunk.) "You make me feel dirty and tired and old!"

'I turned against the wall. The policemen and the people

in the street collected. I was cold and terribly ashamed. I said, "Do you mean that?" And she said she meant it. She put her head down on one of the officers' shoulders. She was drunk. He had her by her wrist, one hand on her behind. She did not say anything about that, because she did not notice, and kept spitting horrible things at me. Then I walked away very fast. My head seemed to be in a large place. She began running after me. I kept on walking. I was cold, and I was not miserable any more. She caught me by the shoulder and went against me, grinning. She stumbled and I held her, and she said, seeing a poor wretched beggar of a whore, "Give her some money, all of it!" She threw the francs into the street and bent down over the filthy baggage and began stroking her hair, grey with the dust of years, saying, "They are all God-forsaken, and you most of all, because they don't want you to have your happiness. They don't want you to drink. Well, here, drink! I give you money and permission! These women – they are all like her," she said with fury. "They are all good – they want to save us!" She sat down beside her.

'It took me and the *garçon* half an hour to get her up and into the lobby, and when I got her that far she began fighting, so that suddenly, without thinking, but out of weariness and misery I struck her; and at that she started, and smiled and went up the stairs with me without complaint. She sat up in bed and ate eggs and called me, "Angel! Angel!" and ate my eggs too, and turned over, and went to sleep. Then I kissed her, holding her hands and feet, and I said: "Die now, so you will be quiet, so you will not be touched again by dirty hands; so you will not take my heart and your body and let them be nosed by dogs – die now, then you will be mine forever." (What right has anyone to that?)' She stopped. 'She was mine only when she was drunk, Matthew, and had passed out. That's the terrible thing, that finally she was mine only when she was dead drunk. All the time I didn't believe her life was as it was and yet, the fact that I didn't proves something is wrong with me. I saw her always like a tall child who had grown up the length of the infant's gown, walking and needing help and safety; because she was in her own nightmare. I tried to come between and save her, but, I was like a shadow in her dream that could never reach her in time, as the cry of the sleeper has no echo, myself echo struggling to answer; she was like a new shadow walking perilously close to the outer curtain, and I was going mad because I was awake and seeing it, unable to reach it, unable to strike people down from it; and it moving, almost unwalking, with the face saintly and idiotic.

'And then that day I'll remember all my life, when I said: "It is over now," she was asleep and I struck her awake. I saw her come awake and turn befouled before me, she who had managed in that sleep to keep whole. Matthew, for God's sake, say something, you are awful enough to say it, say something! I didn't know, I didn't know that it was to be me who was to do the terrible thing! No rot had touched her until then, and there before my eyes I saw her corrupt all at once and withering, because I had struck her sleep away, and I went mad and I've been mad ever since; and there's nothing to do; nothing! You must say something, oh, God, say something!'

'Stop it! Stop it!' he cried. 'Stop screaming! Put your hands down! Stop it! You were a "good woman", and so a bitch on a high plane, the only one able to kill yourself and Robin! Robin was outside the "human type" – a wild thing caught in a woman's skin, monstrously alone, monstrously vain; like the paralysed man in Coney Island – (take away a

131

man's conformity and you take away his remedy) – who had to lie on his back in a box, but the box was lined with velvet, his fingers jewelled with stones, and suspended over him where he could never take his eyes off, a sky-blue mounted mirror, for he wanted to enjoy his own "difference". Robin is not in your life, you are in her dream, you'll never get out of it. And why does Robin feel innocent? Every bed she leaves, without caring, fills her heart with peace and happiness. She has made her "escape" again. That's why she can't "put herself in another's place", she herself is the only "position"; so she resents it when you reproach her with what she had done. She knows she is innocent because she can't do anything in relation to any one but herself. You almost caught hold of her, but she put you cleverly away by making you the Madonna. What was your patience and terror worth all these years if you couldn't keep them for her sake? Did you have to learn wisdom on her knees?

'Oh, for God's sweet sake, couldn't you stand not learning your lesson? Because the lesson we learn is always by giving death and a sword to our lover. You are full to the brim with pride, but I am an empty pot going forward, saying my prayers in a dark place; because I know no one loves, I, least of all, and that no one loves me, that's what makes most people so passionate and bright, because they want to love and be loved, when there is only a bit of lying in the ear to make the ear forget what time is compiling. So I, Dr O'Connor, say, creep by, softly, softly, and don't learn anything, because it's always learned of another person's body; take action in your heart and be careful whom you love – for a lover who dies, no matter how forgotten, will take somewhat of you to the grave. Be humble like the dust, as God intended, and crawl, and finally you'll crawl to the end of the gutter and not be missed and not much remembered.'

'Sometimes,' Nora said, 'she would sit at home all day, looking out of the window or playing with her toys, trains, and animals and cars to wind up, and dolls and marbles and soldiers. But all the time she was watching me, to see that no one called, that the bell did not ring, that I got no mail, nor anyone hallooing in the court, though she knew that none of these things could happen. My life was hers.

'Sometimes, if she got tight by evening, I would find her standing in the middle of the room, in boy's clothes, rocking from foot to foot, holding the doll she had given us – "our child" – high above her head, as if she would cast it down, a look of fury on her face. And one time, about three in the morning when she came in, she was angry because for once I had not been there all the time, waiting. She picked up the doll and hurled it to the floor and put her foot on it, crushing her heel into it; and then, as I came crying behind her, she kicked it, its china head all in dust, its skirt shivering and stiff, whirling over and over across the floor, its blue bow now over, now under.'

The doctor brought his palms together. 'If you, who are bloodthirsty with love, had left her alone, what? Would a lost girl in Dante's time have been a lost girl still, and he had turned his eyes on her? She would have been remembered, and the remembered put on the dress of immunity. Do you think that Robin had no right to fight you with her only weapon? She saw in you that fearful eye that would make her a target forever. Have not girls done as much for the doll – the doll – yes, target of things past and to come? The last doll, given to age, is the girl who should have been a boy, and the boy who should have been a girl! The love of that last doll was foreshadowed in that love of the first. The

133

doll and the immature have something right about them, the doll, because it resembles, but does not contain life, and the third sex, because it contains life but resembles the doll. The blessed face! It should be seen only in profile, otherwise it is observed to be the conjunction of the identical cleaved halves of sexless misgiving! Their kingdom is without precedent. Why do you think I have spent near fifty years weeping over bars but because I am one of them! The uninhabited angel! That is what you have always been hunting!'

'Perhaps, Matthew, there are devils? Who knows if there are devils? Perhaps they have set foot in the uninhabited. Was I her devil trying to bring her comfort? I enter my dead and bring no comfort, not even in my dreams. There in my sleep was my grandmother, who I loved more than anyone, tangled in the grave grass, and flowers blowing about and between her; lying there in the grave, in the forest, in a coffin of glass, and flying low, my father who is still living; low going and into the grave beside her, his head thrown back and his curls lying out, struggling with her death terribly, and me, stepping about its edges, walking and wailing without a sound; round and round, seeing them struggling with that death as if they were struggling with the sea and my life; I was weeping and unable to do anything or take myself out of it. There they were, in the grave glass, and the grave water and the grave flowers and the grave time, one living and one dead and one asleep. It went on forever, though it had stopped, my father stopped beating and just lay there floating beside her, immovable, yet drifting in a tight place. And I woke up and still it was going on; it went down into the dark earth of my waking as if I were burying them with the earth of my lost sleep. This I have done to my father's mother, dreaming through my father, and have tormented them with my tears and with my dreams: for all of us die over again in somebody's sleep. And this, I have done to Robin: it is only through me that she will die over and over, and it is only through me, of all my family, that my grandfather dies, over and over. I woke and got up out of bed and putting my hands between my knees I said, "What was that dream saying, for God's sake, what was that dream?" For it was for me also.'

Suddenly, Dr Matthew O'Connor said: 'It's my mother without argument I want!' And then, in his loudest voice he roared: 'Mother of God! I wanted to be your son – the unknown beloved second would have done!'

'Oh, Matthew. I don't know how to go. I don't know which way to turn! Tell her, if you ever see her, that it is always with her in my arms – forever it will be that way until we die. Tell her to do what she must, but not to forget.'

'Tell her yourself,' said the doctor, 'or sit in your own trouble silently, if you like, it's the same with ermines – those fine yellow ermines that women pay such a great price for – how did they get that valuable colour? By sitting in bed all their lives and pissing the sheets, or weeping in their own way. It's the same with persons; they are only of value when they have laid themselves open to "nuisance"– their own, and the world's. Ritual itself constitutes an instruction. So we come back to the place from which I set out; pray to the good God, she will keep you. Personally I call her "she" because of the way she made me; it somehow balances the mistake.' He got up and crossed to the window. 'That priceless galaxy of misinformation called the mind, harnessed to that stupendous and threadbare glomerate compulsion called the soul, ambling down the almost obliterated bridle path of Well and Ill, fortuitously planned – is the holy Habeas Corpus, the manner in which the body is brought before the judge – still – in the end Robin will wish you in a nunnery where what she loved is, by surroundings, made safe, because as you are you keep "bringing her up", as cannons bring up the dead from deep water.'

'In the end,' Nora said, 'they came to me, the girls Robin had driven frantic – to me, for comfort!' She began to laugh. 'My God,' she said, 'the women I've held upon my knees!'

'Women,' the doctor said, 'were born on the knees, that's why I've never been able to do anything about them, I'm on my own so much of the time.'

'Suddenly, I knew what all my life had been, Matthew, what I hoped Robin was – the secure torment. We can hope for nothing greater, except hope. If I asked her, crying, not to go out, she would go just the same, richer in her heart because I had touched it, as she was going down the stairs.'

'Lions grow their manes and foxes their teeth on that bread,' interpolated the doctor.

'In the beginning, when I tried to stop her from drinking and staying out all night, and from being defiled, she would say – "Ah, I feel so pure and gay!" as if the ceasing of that abuse was her only happiness and peace of mind; and so I struggled with her as with the coils of my own most obvious heart, holding her by the hair, striking her against my knees, as some people in trouble strike their hands too softly; and as if it were a game, she raised and dropped her head against my lap, as a child bounces in a crib to enter excitement, even if it were someone gutted on a dagger. I thought I loved her for her sake, and I found it was for my own.'

'I know,' said the doctor, 'there you were sitting up high and fine, with a rose-bush up your arse.'

136

She looked at him, then she smiled. 'How should you know?'

'I'm a lady in no need of insults,' said the doctor. 'I know.'

'Yes,' she said. 'You know what none of us know until we have died. You were dead in the beginning.'

The twilight was falling. About the street lamps there was a heavy mist. 'Why don't you rest now?' asked the doctor. 'Your body is coming to it, you are forty and the body has a politic too, and a life of its own that you like to think is yours. I heard a spirit mew once, but I knew it was a mystery eternally moving outward and on, and not my own.'

'I know,' she said, '*now*.' Suddenly, she began to cry, holding her hands. 'Matthew,' she said, 'have you ever loved someone and it became yourself?'

For a moment he did not answer. Taking up the decanter, he held it to the light.

'Robin can go anywhere, do anything,' Nora continued, 'because she forgets, and I nowhere, because I remember.' She came toward him. 'Matthew,' she said, 'you think I have always been like this. Once I was remorseless, but this is another love – it goes everywhere, there is no place for it to stop – it rots me away. How could she tell me when she had nothing to tell that wasn't evidence against herself?'

The doctor said, 'You know as well as I do that we were born twelve, and brought up thirteen, and that some of us lived. My brother, whom I had not seen in four years, and loved the most of all, died, and who was it but me my mother wanted to talk to? Not those who had seen him last, but me who had seen him best, as if my memory of him were himself; and because you forget Robin the best, it's to you she turns. She comes trembling, and defiant, and belligerent, all right – that you may give her back to herself again as you have forgotten her – you are the only one strong enough to have listened to the prosecution, your life; and to have built back the amazing defence, your heart!

'The scalpel and the Scriptures have taught me that little I did not already know. And I was doing well enough,' he snapped, 'until you came along and kicked my stone over, and out I came, all moss and eyes; and here I sit, as naked as only those things can be, whose houses have been torn away from them to make a holiday, and it my only skin – labouring to comfort you. Am I supposed to render up my paradise – that splendid acclimatation – for the comfort of weeping women and howling boys? Look at Felix now, what kind of a Jew is that? Screaming up against tradition like a bat against a window-pane, high up over the town, his child a boy weeping "o'er graves of hope and pleasure gone".

'Ah, yes – I love my neighbour. Like a rotten apple to a rotten apple's breast affixed we go down together, nor is there a hesitation in that decay, for when I sense such, there I apply the breast the firmer, that he may rot as quickly as I, in which he stands in dire need or I miscalculate the cry. I, who am done sooner than any fruit! The heat of his suppuration has mingled his core with mine, and wrought my own to the zenith before its time. The encumbrance of myself I threw away long ago, that breast to breast I might go with my failing friends. And do they love me for it? They do not. So have I divorced myself, not only because I was born as ugly as God dared premeditate, but because with propinquity and knowledge of trouble I have damaged my own value. And death – have you thought of death? What risk do you take? Do you know which dies first, you or she? And which is the sorrier part, head or feet? I say, with that good Sir Don, the feet. Any man can look upon the head in death, but no man can look upon the feet. They are most awfully tipped up from the earth. I've thought of that also. Do you think, for Christ's sweet sake,' he shouted suddenly, 'that I am so happy that you should cry down my neck? Do you think there is no lament in this world, but your own? Is there no bread that does not come proffered with bitter butter? I, as good a Catholic as they make, have embraced every confection of hope, and yet I know well, for all our outcry and struggle, we shall be for the next generation not the massive dung fallen from the dinosaur, but the little speck left of a humming-bird; so as well sing our *Chi vuol la Zingarella* (how women love it!) while I warble my *Sonate au Crépuscule*, throwing in *Der Erlkönig* for good measure, not to mention *Who is Sylvia?* Who is anybody!

'Oh,' he cried. 'A broken heart have you! I have falling arches, flying dandruff, a floating kidney, shattered nerves *and* a broken heart! But do I scream that an eagle has me by the balls or has dropped his oyster on my heart? Am I going forward screaming that it hurts, that my mind goes back, or holding my guts as if they were a coil of knives? Yet you are screaming, and drawing your lip and putting your hand out and turning round and round! Do I wail to the mountains of the trouble I have had in the valley, or to every stone of the way it broke my bones, or of every lie, how it went down into my belly and built a nest to hatch me to my death there? Isn't everyone in the world peculiarly swung and me the craziest of the lot – so that I come dragging and squealing, like a heifer on the way to slaughter, knowing his cries have only half a rod to go, protesting his death – as his death has only a rod to go to protest his screaming? Do you walk high Heaven without shoes? Are you the only person with a bare foot pressed down on a rake? Oh, you poor blind cow! Keep out of my feathers; you ruffle me the wrong way and flit about, stirring my misery! What end is sweet? Are the ends of the hair sweet when you come to number them?'

'Listen,' Nora said. 'You've got to listen! She would come back to me after a night all over the city and lie down beside me and she would say, "I want to make everyone happy," and her mouth was drawn down. "I want everyone to be gay, gay. Only you," she said, holding me, "only you, you mustn't be gay or happy, not like that, it's not for you, only for everyone else in the world." She knew she was driving me insane with misery and fright; only,' she went on, 'she couldn't do anything because she was a long way off and waiting to begin. It's for that reason she hates everyone near her. It's why she falls into everything, like someone in a dream. It's why she wants to be loved and left alone, all at the same time. She would kill the world to get at herself if the world were in the way, and it *is* in the way. A shadow was falling on her – mine – and it was driving her out of her wits.'

She began to walk again. 'I have been loved,' she said, 'by something strange, and it has forgotten me.' Her eyes were fixed and she seemed to be talking to herself. 'It was *me* made her hair stand on end, because I loved her. She turned bitter because I made her fate colossal. She wanted darkness in her mind – to throw a shadow over what she was powerless to alter – her dissolute life, her life at night; and I, I dashed it down. We will never have it out now,' Nora said. 'It's too late. There is no last reckoning for those who have loved too long, so for me there is no end. Only I can't, I can't wait forever!' she said frantically. 'I can't live without my heart!

'In the beginning, after Robin went away with Jenny to America, I searched for her in the ports. Not literally, in another way. Suffering is the decay of the heart; all that we have loved becomes the "forbidden", when we have not understood it all, as the pauper is the rudiment of a city, knowing something of the city, which the city, for its own destiny, wants to forget. So the lover must go against nature to find love. I sought Robin in Marseilles, in Tangier, in Naples, to understand her, to do away with my terror. I said to myself, I will do what she has done, I will love what she has loved, then I will find her again. At first it seemed that all I should have to do would be to become "debauched", to find the girls that she had loved; but I found that they were only little girls that she had forgotten. I haunted the cafés where Robin had lived her night-life; I drank with the men, I danced with the women, but all I knew was that others had slept with my lover and my child. For Robin is incest too, that is one of her powers. In her, past-time records, and past time is relative to us all. Yet not being the family she is more present than the family. A relative is in the foreground only when it is born, when it suffers and when it dies, unless it becomes one's lover, then it must be everything, as Robin was; yet not as much as she, for she was like a relative found in another generation. I thought, "I will do something that she will never be able to forgive, then we can begin again as strangers." But the sailor got no further than the hall. He said: "*Mon dieu, il y a deux chevaux de bois dans la chambre à coucher.*"'

'Christ!' muttered the doctor.

'So,' Nora continued, 'I left Paris. I went through the streets of Marseilles, the waterfront of Tangier, the *basso porto* of Naples. In the narrow streets of Naples, ivies and flowers were growing over the broken-down walls. Under enormous staircases, rising open to the streets, beggars lay sleeping beside images of St Gennaro; girls going into the churches to pray were calling out to boys in the squares. In open doorways night-lights were burning all day before gaudy prints of the Virgin. In one room that lay open to the alley, before a bed covered with a cheap heavy satin comforter, in the semi-darkness, a young girl sat on a chair, leaning over its back, one arm across it, the other hanging at her side, as if half of her slept; and half of her suffered. When she saw me she laughed, as children do, in embarrassment. Looking from her to the Madonna behind the candles, I knew that the image, to her, was what I had been to Robin, not a saint at all, but a fixed dismay, the space between the human and the holy head, the arena of the "indecent" eternal. At that moment I stood in the centre of eroticism and death, death that makes the dead smaller, as a lover we are beginning to forget dwindles and wastes; for love and life are a bulk of which the body and heart can be drained, and I knew in that bed Robin should have put me down. In that bed we would have forgotten our lives in the extremity of memory, moulted our parts, as fingers in the wax works are moulted down to their story, so we would have broken-down to our love.'

The doctor stood up. He staggered as he reached for his hat and coat. He stood in confused and unhappy silence – he moved toward the door. Holding the knob in his hand he turned toward her. Then he went out.

The doctor, walking with his coat-collar up, entered the Café de la Mairie du VIe. He stood at the bar and ordered a drink, looking at the people in the close, smoke-blue room, he said to himself, 'Listen!' Nora troubled him, the life of Nora and the lives of the people in his life. 'The way of a man in a fog!' he said. He hung his umbrella on the bar ledge. 'To think is to be sick,' he said to the barman. The barman nodded.

The people in the café waited for what the doctor would say, knowing that he was drunk and that he would talk; in great defaming sentences his betrayals came up; no one ever knew what was truth and what was not. 'If you really want to know how hard a prize-fighter hits,' he said, looking around, 'you have got to walk into the circle of his fury and be carried out by the heels, not by the count.'

Someone laughed. The doctor turned slowly. 'So safe as all that?' he asked sarcastically; 'so damned safe? Well, wait until you get in gaol and find yourself slapping the bottoms of your feet for misery.'

He put his hand out for his drink – muttering to himself: 'Matthew, you have never been in time with any man's life and you'll never be remembered at all, God save the vacancy! The finest instrument goes wrong in time – that's all, the instrument gets broken, and I must remember that when everyone is strange; it's the instrument gone flat. Lapidary, engrave that on my stone when Matthew is all over and lost in a field.' He looked around. 'It's the instrument, gentlemen, that has lost its G string, otherwise he'd be playing a fine tune; otherwise he'd still be passing his wind with the wind of the north – otherwise touching his billycock!'

'Only the scorned and the ridiculous make good stories,' he added angrily, seeing the habitués smiling, 'so you can imagine when you'll get told! Life is only long enough for one trade; try that one!'

An unfrocked priest, a stout pale man with woman's hands, on which were many rings, a friend of the doctor's, called him and asked him to have a drink. The doctor came, carefully bringing his umbrella and hat. The priest said: 'I've always wanted to know whether you were ever *really* married or not.'

'Should I know that?' inquired the doctor. 'I've *said* I was married and I gave the girl a name and had children by her, then, presto! I killed her off as lightly as the death of swans. And was I reproached for that story? I was. Because even your friends regret weeping for a myth, as if that were not practically the fate of all the tears in the world! What if the girl *was* the wife of my brother and the children my brother's children? When I laid her down her limbs were as handsome and still as two May boughs from the cutting – did he do as much for her? I imagined about her in my heart as pure as a French print, a girl all of a little bosom and a birdcage, lying back down comfortable with the sea for a background and a rope of roses to hold her. Has any man's wife been treated better than that? Who says she might not have been mine, and the children also? Who for that matter,' he said with violence, 'says they are not mine? Is not a brother his brother also, the one blood cut up in lengths, one called Michael and the other Matthew? Except that people get befuddled seeing them walk in different directions? Who's to say that I'm not my brother's wife's husband and that his children were not fathered in my lap? Is it not to his honour that he strikes me as myself? And when she died, did my weeping make his weeping less?'

The ex-priest said, 'Well, there's something in that, still I like to know what is what.'

'You do, do you?' said the doctor. 'Well then, that's why you are where you are now, right down in the mud without a feather to fly with, like the ducks in Golden Gate park – the largest park in captivity – everybody with their damnable kindness having fed them all the year round to their ruin because when it comes time for their going south they are all a bitter consternation, being too fat and heavy to rise off the water, and, my God, how they flop and struggle all over the park in autumn, crying and tearing their hair out because their nature is weighed down with bread and their migration stopped, by crumbs. You wring your hands to see it, and that's another illustration of love; in the end you are too heavy to move with the greediness in your stomach. And,' said the doctor, 'it would be the same with me if I'd let it, what with the wind at the one end and the cyclone at the other. Yet there are some that I have neglected for my spirit's sake – the old yeomen of the Guard and the beefeaters of the Tower because of their cold kidneys and grey hairs, and the kind of boy who only knows two existences – himself in a mirror – back and front.' He was very drunk now. He looked about the café. He caught someone nudging someone. He looked up at the ex-priest and cursed. 'What people! All queer in a terrible way. There were a couple of queer *good* people once in this world – but none of you,' he said, addressing the room, 'will ever know them. You think you are all studded with diamonds, don't you! Well, part the diamonds and you'll find slug's meat. My God,' he said, turning around, 'when I think!' He began to pound the table with his glass. 'May they all be damned! The people in my life who have made my life miserable, coming to me to learn of degradation and the night. Nora, beating her head against her heart, sprung over, her mind closing her life up like a heel on a fan, rotten to the bone for love of Robin. My God, how that woman can hold on to an idea! And that old sandpiper, Jenny! Oh, it's a grand bad story, and who says I'm a betrayer? I say, tell the story of the world to the world!'

'A sad and a corrupt age,' the ex-priest said.

Matthew O'Connor called for another drink. 'What do they all come to me for? Why do they all tell me everything then expect it to lie hushed in me, like a rabbit gone home to die? And that Baron Felix, hardly muttered a word in his life, and yet his silence breeds like scum on a pond; and that boy of his, Guido, by Robin, trying to see across the Danube with the tears in his eyes, Felix holding on to his hand and the boy holding on to the image of the Virgin on a darkening red ribbon, feeling its holy lift out of the metal and calling it mother; and me not even knowing which direction my end is coming from. So, when Felix said to me, "Is the child infirm?" I said, "Was the Mad King of Bavaria infirm?" I'm not one to cut the knot by drowning myself in any body of water, not even the print of a horse's hoof, no matter how it has been raining.'

People had begun to whisper and the waiters moved closer, watching. The ex-priest was smiling to himself, but O'Connor did not seem to see or hear anything but his own heart. 'Some people,' he said, 'take off head-first into *any* body of water and six glasses later someone in Haarlem gets typhoid from drinking their misery. God, take my hand and get me up out of this great argument – the more you go against your nature, the more you will know of it – hear me, heaven! I've done, and been everything that I didn't want to be or do – Lord, put the light out – so I stand here, beaten up and mauled and weeping, knowing I am not what I thought I was, a good man doing wrong, but the wrong man doing nothing much, and I wouldn't be telling you about it if I weren't talking to myself. I talk too much, because I have been made so miserable by what you are keeping hushed. I'm an old worn out lioness, a coward in my corner, for the sake of my bravery I've never been one thing that I am, to find out what I am! Here lies the body of Heaven. The mocking bird howls through the pillars of Paradise, oh, Lord! Death in Heaven lies couched on a mackerel sky, on her breast a helmet and at her feet a foal with a silent marble mane. Nocturnal sleep is heavy on her eyes.'

'Funny little man,' someone said, 'never stops talking – always getting everyone into trouble by excusing them, because he can't excuse himself – the Squatting Beast, coming out at night' – as he broke off, the voice of the doctor was heard: 'And what am I? I'm damned, and carefully public!'

He fumbled for a cigarette, found it and lit it.

'Once upon a time, I was standing listening to a quack hanky-panky of a medicine man saying: "Now, ladies and gentlemen, before I behead the small boy, I will endeavour to entertain you with a few parlour tricks." He had a turban cocked over his eye and a moaning in his left ventricle which was meant to be the whine of Tophet, and a loin-cloth as big as a tent and protecting about as much. Well, he began doing his tricks. He made a tree grow out of his left shoulder and dashed two rabbits out of his cuffs and balanced three eggs on his nose. A priest, standing in the crowd, began to laugh, and a priest laughing always makes me wring my hands with doubt. The other time was when Catherine the Great sent for me to bleed her. She took to the leech with rowdy Saxon abandon, saying: "Let him drink, I've always wanted to be in two places at once!"'

'For heaven's sake,' the ex-priest said. 'Remember your century at least!'

For a moment the doctor looked angry. 'See here,' he said, 'don't interrupt me. The reason I'm so remarkable is that I remember everyone even when they are not about. It's the boys that look as innocent as the bottom of a plate that get you into trouble, not a man with a prehistoric memory.'

'Women can cause trouble too,' the ex-priest said lamely.

'That's another story,' the doctor said. 'What else has

Jenny ever done, and what else has Robin ever done? And Nora, what's she done but cause it, by taking it in at night like a bird-coop? And I myself wish I'd never had a button up my middle – for what I've done and what I've not done all goes back to that – to be recognized, a gem should lie in a wide open field; but I'm all aglitter in the underbrush! If you don't want to suffer you should tear yourself apart. Were not the several parts of Caroline of Hapsburg put in three utterly obvious piles? – her heart in the Augustiner church, her intestines in St Stefan's and what was left of the body in the vault of the Capucines? Saved by separation. But I'm all in one piece! Oh, the new moon!' he said. 'When will she come riding?'

'Drunk and telling the world,' someone said.

The doctor heard but he was too far gone to care, too muddled in his mind to argue, and already weeping.

'Come,' the ex-priest said, 'I'll take you home.'

The doctor waved his arm. 'Revenge is for those who have loved a little, for anything more than that justice is hardly enough. Some day I'm going to Lourdes and scramble in the front row and talk about all of you.' His eyes were almost closed. He opened them and looked about him and a fury came over him. 'Christ Almighty!' he said. 'Why don't they let me alone, all of them?'

The ex-priest repeated, 'Come, I'll take you home.'

The doctor tried to rise. He was exceedingly drunk and now extremely angry all at once. His umbrella fell to the floor with the crash of a glass as he swung his arm upward against the helping hand. 'Get out! Get out!' he said. 'What a damnable year, what a bloody time! How did it happen, where did it come from?'

He began to scream with sobbing laughter. 'Talking to me – all of them – sitting on me as heavy as a truck horse –

talking! Love falling buttered side down, fate falling arse up! Why doesn't anyone know when everything is over, except me? That fool Nora, holding on by her teeth, going back to find Robin! And Felix – eternity is only just long enough for a Jew! But there's someone else – who was it, damn it all – who was it? I've known everyone,' he said, 'everyone!' He came down upon the table with all his weight, his arms spread, his head between them, his eyes wide and open and crying, staring along the table where the ash blew and fluttered with his gasping breath. 'For Christ's sweet sake!' he said, and his voice was a whisper, 'Now that you have all heard what you wanted to hear, can't you let me loose now, let me go? I've not only lived my life for nothing, but I've told it for nothing – abominable among the filthy people – I know, it's all over, everything's over, and nobody knows it but me – drunk as a fiddler's bitch – lasted too long –' He tried to get to his feet, gave it up. 'Now,' he said, 'the end – mark my words – now *nothing, but wrath and weeping*!'

CHAPTER EIGHT

The Possessed

When Robin, accompanied by Jenny Petherbridge, arrived in New York, she seemed distracted. She would not listen to Jenny's suggestion that they should make their home in the country. She said a hotel was 'good enough'. Jenny could do nothing with her; it was as if the motive power which had directed Robin's life, her day as well as her night, had been crippled. For the first week or two she would not go out, then, thinking herself alone, she began to haunt the terminals, taking trains into different parts of the country, wandering without design, going into many out-of-the-way churches, sitting in the darkest corner, or standing against the wall, one foot turned toward the toe of the other, her hands folded at their length, her head bent. As she had taken the Catholic vow long before, now she came into church as one renouncing something; her hands before her face, she knelt, her teeth against her palm, fixed in an unthinking stop as one who hears of death suddenly; death that cannot form until the shocked tongue has given its permission. Moving like a housewife come to set straight disorder in an unknown house, she came forward with a lighted taper, and setting it up, she turned, drawing on her thick white gloves, and with her slow headlong step, left the church. A moment later Jenny, who had followed her, looking about to be sure that she was unobserved, darted up to the sconce, snatched the candle from its spike, blew it out; relit it and set it back.

Robin walked the open country in the same manner, pulling at the flowers, speaking in a low voice to the animals. Those that came near, she grasped, straining their fur back until their eyes were narrowed and their teeth bare, her own teeth showing as if her hand were upon her own neck.

Because Robin's engagements were with something unseen; because in her speech and in her gestures there was a desperate anonymity, Jenny became hysterical. She accused Robin of a 'sensuous communion with unclean spirits'. And in putting her wickedness into words she struck herself down. She did not understand anything Robin felt or did, which was more unendurable than her absence. Jenny walked up and down her darkened hotel room, crying and stumbling.

Robin now headed up into Nora's part of the country. She circled closer and closer. Sometimes she slept in the woods; the silence that she had caused by her coming was broken again by insect and bird flowing back over her intrusion, which was forgotten in her fixed stillness, obliterating her as a drop of water is made anonymous by the pond into which it has fallen. Sometimes she slept on a bench in the decaying chapel (she brought some of her things here) but she never went further. One night she woke up to the barking, far off, of Nora's dog. As she had frightened the woods into silence by her breathing, the barking of the dog brought her up rigid and still.

Half an acre away Nora, sitting by a kerosene lamp, raised her head. The dog was running about the house; she heard him first on one side, then the other; he whined as he ran; barking and whining she heard him further and further away. Nora bent forward, listening; she began to shiver. After a moment she got up, unlocking the doors and windows. Then she sat down, her hands on her knees; but she couldn't wait. She went out. The night was well advanced. She no longer heard the dog, but she kept on. A level above her she heard things rustling in the grass, the briars made her stumble, but she did not call.

At the top of the hill she could see, rising faintly against the sky, the weather-beaten white of the chapel; a light ran the length of the door. She began to run, cursing and crying, and blindly, without warning, plunged into the jamb of the chapel door.

On a contrived altar, before a Madonna, two candles were burning. Their light fell across the floor and the dusty benches. Before the image lay flowers and toys. Standing before them in her boy's trousers was Robin. Her pose, startled and broken, was caught at the point where her hand had reached almost to the shoulder, and at the moment Nora's body struck the wood, Robin began going down. Sliding down she went; down, her hair swinging, her arms held out, and the dog stood there, rearing back, his forelegs slanting; his paws trembling under the trembling of his rump, his hackle standing; his mouth open, his tongue slung sideways over his sharp bright teeth; whining and waiting. And down she went, until her head swung against his; on all fours now, dragging her knees. The veins stood out in her neck, under her ears, swelled in her arms, and wide and throbbing rose up on her fingers as she moved forward.

The dog, quivering in every muscle, sprang back, his lips drawn, his tongue a stiff curving terror in his mouth; moved backward, back, as she came on, whimpering too now, coming forward, her head turned completely sideways, grinning and whimpering. Backed now into the farthest corner, the dog reared as if to avoid something that troubled him to such agony that he seemed to be rising from the floor; then he stopped, clawing sideways at the wall, his forepaws lifted and sliding. Then, head down, dragging her forelocks in the dust, she struck against his side. He let loose one howl of misery and bit at her, dashing about her, barking, and as he sprang on either side of her he kept his head toward her, dashing his rump now this side, now that, of the wall.

Then she began to bark also, crawling after him – barking in a fit of laughter, obscene and touching. The dog began to cry, running with her, head-on with her head, as if to circumvent her; soft and slow his feet went. He ran this way and that, low down in his throat crying, and she grinning and crying with him; crying in shorter and shorter spaces, moving head to head, until she gave up, lying out, her hands beside her, her face turned and weeping; and the dog too gave up then, and lay down, his eyes bloodshot, his head flat along her knees.